Burning Daylight

Book 3 of The Pandora Chronicles

Rebecca Flynn

ISBN: 978-1-68433-855-3
PUBLISHED BY BLACK ROSE WRITING
www.blackrosewriting.com

Printed in the United States of America
Suggested Retail Price (SRP) $19.95

Black Rose Writing | Texas

Black Rose Writing and its logo are properties of Black Rose Writing, LLC. We use any wholesale or retail pricing, inventory costs, while developing costs, the trading distribution. As a result, the books cost is inexpensively, not meet common expectations.

The author grants the final approval for this literary material.

First printing

This is a work of fiction. Names, characters, businesses, places, events, and incidents are either the products of the author's imagination or used in a fictitious manner. Any resemblance to actual persons, living or dead, or actual events is purely coincidental.

ISBN: 978-1-68433-895-5
PUBLISHED BY BLACK ROSE WRITING
www.blackrosewriting.com

Printed in the United States of America
Suggested Retail Price (SRP) $18.95

Burning Daylight is printed in Calluna

*As a planet-friendly publisher, Black Rose Writing does its best to eliminate unnecessary waste to reduce paper usage and energy costs, while never compromising the reading experience. As a result, the final word count vs. page count may not meet common expectations.

To my big sister, Samantha.

Life has never really seemed to take us in the direction we thought we'd be heading. I didn't think I'd graduate before you and I doubt you ever thought you'd be working in the field I studied. We played together, we fought, we hung out, we argued. There have been days that I wondered if you ever even wanted me to be your sister. But then there are days when those moments just fade away. We've been through a lot together. Good or bad, it's been together and that's all that matters. Thank you for being my sister.

Burning Daylight

Prologue

A rumble rippled under the hot sands of Egypt. A warm breeze blew across the sand dunes and passed the pyramids. Scorpions skittered around and buried themselves beneath the surface. Sidewinders twisted and curved their way through the darkness.

The moon, full and bright, lit the peaks and left the valleys painted in black. A soft voice whispered across the still air. There was a yawn as the voice mumbled incoherently and groaned.

Vibrations shook the walls of a dark room buried beneath the cold sand.

"What now?" a female voice grumbled.

Bits of metal clanked against metal as the room shook again.

"You trap me and promise me darkness and silence," she growled. "And then you disturb my sleep!"

The walls shook from the echo of her bellow. Sand poured down over her body again.

A steady rumble began. Slowly, it increased in intensity until the vibrations were so violent that her body was thrown to the floor. Metal and sand sprayed her and buried half her body.

"You dare to disrespect me!" she shouted, unsure where the attack had come from. "Do you even know who I am?" She stood up in the darkness. The metal tumbled down into the already massive pile beneath her feet. Lightning sparked and crackled from her jaws. The room lit up in flashes. "I am Tiamet!" she growled. "I am a goddess! The Tigres and Euphrates flow freely because of me! I am the mother of dragons! You will show me the respect I deserve!"

The vibrations turned into a quake. The ground shifted all around her. The walls moved and scraped. A loud crack echoed in the chamber and one of the walls collapsed. Sand poured into the room quickly. Tiamet spun around and howled as her treasure disappeared.

"No!" she shouted. "You will not take what is mine! Everything is mine! You are nothing without me!" Lightning shot out from her jaws and struck the sand. Glass spires formed in the site of impact. "I will destroy you!" She heaved and howled as more and more spires shot up around her.

The vibrations subsided and the sands slowed. The gold coins sat quietly and safely beneath a layer of glass. She looked around and growled. Her eyes stopped on the broken wall. A smile spread across her jaws as tiny sparks danced between her massive teeth. "It would appear that I am free. The time has come to step out into this wretched world again and see what it has become."

The first claw slipped out into the moonlight. It glowed and shifted into a slender hand. Tiamet pulled her body from her wrecked prison and breathed in the crisp night air. Her ebony skin glowed with a soft inner light. She smiled. "I am finally free. I must find my mate. Together, our race will be reborn."

Chapter 1

Haydeez huffed and growled in frustration. A horde of bugs scattered and burrowed into the ground around her feet. "I need bug spray," she grumbled. "This is getting ridiculous."

"Find the heart of the beast, love. You need to trap the heart for it to work. Bug spray isn't enough when you're trying to kill thousands," Linx answered. Flames belched from the muzzle of his weapon as he sprayed the creature in front of him. "Why won't you die?" he yelled.

"It's already dead. You just have to make it realize that," Haydeez said. "Dust to dust, Linx."

Fire tore through the dry, ragged fabric wrapped around the long dead body. It howled and reached for Linx. Flames spread through the cloth quickly. The smell of rotted, burnt flesh accosted his nostrils. The creature wriggled and screamed which only aided in the spread of the blaze.

"Found it!" Linx shouted. "She's been quite busy lately."

Haydeez grunted. "Well, she said she needed power. All we're doing is helping her. But if we don't kill these stupid things, they'll kill people. But if we don't stop her, it won't matter anyway!" She yelled in frustration. "We're just building up our opponent." She stomped her feet as the beetles scurried away again. "Ugh! I hate you!"

The beetles piled on top of each other. Their tiny legs linked together like pieces of chainmail. When the last body fell into place, a human figure stood before her. The bugs shifted to form a demented smile. "I feel nothing for you," it clicked and vibrated. "My only desire is to strip you of your flesh and feed on your insides until even your bones have been consumed." It clicked again, like the sound of tiny scarab feet on stone. The creature laughed and swayed.

A burgundy shell stood out against a sea of black. "Found you," she growled.

The creature moved to cover its heart but Haydeez had already seen what she needed. With a jar in her hand, she jumped forward and thrust her empty hand through the mass of beetles. It felt like cold steel. They scraped up her arm like a serrated blade. Her fingertips touched the heart. It was warm, unlike the black shells. She clamped down and yanked it free.

The creature howled in pain. "Not what you expected to happen, is it?" she asked the creature. The heart hit the bottom of the jar with a jingle. Haydeez snapped the lid in place and shook the jar. She watched the beetle bounce around for a moment.

On the underside was that all too familiar mark. "I can only hope that this thing isn't important enough to give you a lot of power," she mumbled. Her fingers moved to a little pump and squeezed. "I hope you feel this. That would be poison. Your heart is dying."

The creature grabbed its chest, took a few steps, and roared as it attempted to grab the jar from Haydeez. The only movement it could muster was a weak flail as it swung its arm at her. Scarabs began to tumble off and sprinkle the floor. Their lifeless little bodies curled in on themselves with their feet in the air.

Haydeez stood over the empty shells for another moment to make sure they had all died. "I really hate bugs." She held up the jar and shook the heart. "Guess you felt that. Well, that's one more creature out of the mix. How many does that make now? I think I lost track."

Linx grunted. "I think we're up to about a dozen now, unless we count each individual little scarab," he joked. "Want to count them all, love?"

Haydeez scoffed. "Yeah, I'll get right on that. I can leave all these little dead guys on the ground and just take the heart, right? I don't have to collect all of them, do I? No, I can just keep the heart. Should be fine," she said to herself. "Probably need something to keep it in."

"Just keep it in the jar, love," Linx chimed in between grunts. "Once she sucks out the life from that thing, it won't matter what we do with it. It'll probably just shrivel up and..."

"Then, it turns back into a human," Haydeez interrupted. Her eyes fell on the now dead man that took the place of tens of thousands of scarabs, a hole in the middle of his chest. "You would think I would remember this stuff after killing off so many already. I guess I'm just getting fried." She glanced at the jar. "Ew. Apparently I now have his actual heart in this jar. Wonderful." The longer she stared at the body, the more she realized that it did not matter to Pandora anymore. She needed power and she would take it from anyone. "She's going to kill them anyway. These people just get to do it sooner," she mumbled. "He can't be more than twenty. He looks like a child. How do you stop someone who is willing to take a child's life? I wonder if she's forcing any of them to actually agree to this." She shook her head. "Do you think anything has changed? Do you think she still needs their permission?"

Linx groaned. "Finally! Bloody hell! That was the last one." He sighed and added, "I'm sure that part hasn't changed. As far as forcing them to agree, if she's desperate enough she probably will. Look, to be honest, that part doesn't really matter. We know she'll get what she wants whether she finds willing participants or not. We need to put as much energy as possible into finding whatever she lets out and killing it and then figuring out how to stop her completely." He paused and looked around the quiet sands. "Just remember there's always something else coming."

Haydeez sighed and shook the jar one last time. The human heart plopped against the sides of the glass. "I need sleep. I'll meet you at the hotel. Don't be too long. I'm ordering food."

"You got it, love. See you soon."

Chapter 2

Linx stared at the clock. He could not believe it was only a little after three in the morning. His body told him to get up and do something but his brain said to stay in bed. He turned his gaze to the ceiling and let out a long slow breath. "Go to sleep," he whispered to himself. "You know you need it. Just close your eyes and sleep."

"Doesn't work. I've already tried that," Haydeez whispered. "For some reason, we're not supposed to sleep right now. Totally unfair." She reached over and turned on the small light on the night stand. "Since we're both awake anyway, do you want to do something?" she asked.

Linx furrowed his brow. "Excuse me?"

"Do you want to do something?" she asked again. "We could go take a walk. We could watch a movie. Do they have a heated pool here? We could take a swim. Something to make me tired so I can sleep."

Linx chuckled. "Wow, I thought you had gone mad for a minute." He propped himself up on his elbows. "Movie sounds good. What do you have in mind?"

Before she could answer, a soft knock came from the other side of the room. They looked at each other warily. "Which door did that come from," Linx asked.

"It better be the bathroom door, or someone is going to have a bad night," she answered as she stood up. She cocked her head to the side and walked over toward the bathroom.

Another soft knock sounded and Haydeez relaxed. She moved her fingers in a pattern on the door and knocked back.

When the door opened, Keeglian stood with a stack of books and papers. "Oh, my apologies. I forgot you were still in another country. Would you prefer that I return at a later time?" he asked.

Haydeez shook her head. "No, that's not necessary. It's not like either of us could sleep anyway. We were just getting ready to watch a movie but if you've got something for us, we're listening." She motioned him into the room.

Keeglian stepped into the hotel room and placed his things on the empty table. He pointed to a thin leather book and said, "This book arrived from a friend of yours. The note said that it should help in your research." He brushed off his vest and cleared his throat. "I hope you're prepared, duckie. It would appear that you will need to find yet another trapped god." He clasped his hands together in front of his body. "You need to find Ra."

Linx flopped down onto his pillow and groaned.

Haydeez smacked her forehead. "Seriously? Come on. We need to find a god to stop her? And what happens if we can't find him? Or worse, what happens if we find him, release him, and he's fine with her destroying the world? What do we do then? Ugh, this is insane!" She plopped onto her bed and huffed.

Linx threw his arm over his face and said, "You had to know something like this was going to happen, love. It's never just a quick little stroll down to the market." He sat up. "So, how do we find Ra? They probably put him somewhere right in front of us. When we finally find him, we'll have to question why we never saw it before," he said.

Keeglian nodded. "You're probably correct. Taking into account that the last one you released was a Celtic god off the coast of Ireland, it would stand to reason that they would put the head of the Egyptian gods somewhere in Egypt. That narrows the window a bit."

"Narrows? Are you kidding me? You do know how massive Egypt is, right?" Haydeez paused. She took a deep breath and let it out slowly. "Sorry. It's not your fault. At least we're in the right place to start looking I suppose. Hopefully this is where we'll stay now. We'll get out there and find him. Then, we'll get him to help us. Then, we'll take out Pandora for good. And maybe if I repeat all that enough times, I might actually convince myself that this will work." She looked up at Keeglian and asked, "So, what do we do when we find him?"

Chapter 3

The full moon cast a cold, clear light over the quiet sands of the desert. A group of five people surrounded a young woman with long black hair. She wore a short black dress with silver stockings that sparkled in the moonlight. The people looked back and forth at each other in confusion as the woman just stood in silence.

"So, you said we were coming out here to party, right? You said you had something that would totally blow our minds," one of the women said. She looked around and added, "So, where is it? It looks like we're just standing out here in the desert."

One man nodded in agreement. "I don't think she's got anything. We came all the way out here for nothing. How long are we supposed to just stand here and watch you stare off into the night? I'm out of here," he said and turned to leave.

Pandora chuckled. "Too late. You have already agreed, my friend." She turned and caught his eyes. Her body had aged almost a decade since the Chimera was killed. She was no longer the youthful child. "Are you ready to feel something you've never felt before?" she asked with a smirk. "You're not going to just walk away from me are you?" She stepped slowly towards him and reached out to take his hand. "I would hate for you to miss all the... excitement." Her finger brushed delicately over the back of his hand. "So, are you ready?"

He stood with his mouth open and eyes wide. His body was frozen in place and he could not take his gaze from her. He nodded slowly.

She shook her finger. "No, no. You have to tell me you want it," she teased.

"I want it. Whatever it is, I want it," he answered quickly.

She giggled. "And what about everyone else?" She turned with his hand still in hers. "Are you all ready? Do you want it too?" she asked.

They all nodded and agreed.

Her eyes closed and she began to mumble. An eerie glow pulsed beneath her dress. She reached down and pulled out the dial and spun each of the rings one at a time.

They gasped.

"What the hell is that?" one asked.

"What are you?" another shouted.

Thunder began to rumble but the sky remained clear. Pandora's hair fluttered as a breeze started to flow around her. She clutched the man's hand as he tried to pull away. Her grip tightened. Words flew quickly from her lips as she spun the dials faster. Every few turns she would stop and touch the gem in the middle.

Panic raced through the group. Two of the people stood trapped in shock while two others turned and tried to run away. The last man scraped at Pandora's hand as he tried feverishly to loosen her grip.

Her eyes flew open. "There is nowhere to go. Once you agree, you're mine," she said coyly. She released his hand and he fell to the ground. The wind whipped around her body. The gem pulsed and shuddered. Shadows spewed from the depths and spread out around her. She laughed. "Welcome, children. Welcome back. These are your new hosts. All have agreed to welcome you inside, to feel things they have never felt before, to become more than what they are. They are yours to take. Choose your body, children. There are enough for each of you." She spread her arms wide and laughed again.

The first shadow slammed into a woman and dropped her to the ground. There was no pause, no moment where the shadow coaxed the human into submission, no quiet song of comfort. The woman screamed in agony as the shadow devoured her on the ground.

Two more shadows swept through the air after the two people who tried to run. They swirled around the people and trapped them. In a moment, the sky went from clear and bright to black. They saw nothing as the shadows constricted around them. They shrieked and shouted for help. The shadows filled the doomed bodies through the open mouths until the sounds finally faded into the darkness.

Another shadow spilled onto the sand like water. It crept toward the man that stood locked to the ground. His heart beat visibly in his chest and he gasped for breath. The shadow crept up his body and wrapped itself around him until it squeezed every inch of him. He choked a few times. The shadow quietly slipped through his lips and began to transform before the man even had the chance to protest.

"Do not tease your host, Sobek. He is the most eager to feel what you offer. He is the most excited about having you inside," she said as she turned to the man on the ground. "Aren't you? After all, you were the first to agree. You came to me and propositioned me first. You seemed agreeable when you thought you had the upper hand but more so when you allowed me to take charge." She reached out to touch his arm. "You would deny yourself this level of ecstasy? Sobek can make you feel stronger and more powerful than you ever will again. Do not fight him and he will be gentle. You have seen the pain the others feel. Their fear made those last moments more painful than a thousand deaths. Accept your fate and feel bliss. It is your choice." She ran her fingers down his arm as he lost himself in her eyes again. "There you go," she whispered. "He will make you whole."

In one swift movement, the shadow clamped down on the man and flowed into him through his nostrils. He inhaled sharply and held his breath. His shoulders stiffened as the darkness filled his body. The man collapsed onto his back and began to convulse.

"Shhh," Pandora whispered. "It will be over quickly."

His body stretched and spasmed. Scales crept over his head where hair should be and his face pulled forward into giant crocodile jaws. A growl formed in his belly and rumbled as his body finished its transformation.

The creature stood and dusted itself off. A golden disc had sprouted from its head and sat upright. A soft glow surrounded the disc as if it had its own celestial power within the subtle depths. "Why have you summoned me here, child? What do you wish of me?" he asked, his voice deep and full of gravel.

She smiled and turned around. What faced her was a group of creatures that stood and began to acclimate themselves to their new bodies. She sighed and admired her work. "I have freed you from your prison for one reason. I am here to destroy man, and you are here to help me. Together we will wipe the world clean of man and reclaim the world that was once ours to control. Some of you may perish. Those are the eventualities when war is declared but just know that when I prevail, the world will be perfect and you will have given your life to create it." She turned to face the crocodile creature. "Dear Sobek, you must take that desire for chaos and spread it everywhere. Let that guide you no matter where you travel. That is all that I ask of you." She motioned for him to leave and bowed slightly in thanks.

Another creature moved forward with the head of a crocodile, shoulders and fore legs of a panther, and back legs of a hippopotamus. When it spoke, a feminine voice shook the sands. "And for the rest of us? You must have plans for us too. Or are we not expected to survive," she stated flatly.

Pandora chuckled. "You are free to do everything that you do best, great Ammit. You are the devourer of souls. I ask that you do that. Once everything is complete, the world will beg for you to take their souls to avoid the fate I have planned for them. Take as many as you like. Good, evil, it does not matter. Take them all." She spread her arms wide. The creature began to leave, a wicked smile on her jaws.

She turned to another creature. At a glance, it appeared to just be a snake. Then, the ground vibrated slightly as the snake shifted. It slithered forward and revealed that there was more body beneath the cool sand. "Dark Apophis, use that which has been gifted to you. Create terrifying earthquakes and thunderstorms. Block out the sun. The once mighty Ra is no longer here to stop you." She swept her arm out and motioned for the serpent creature to leave.

"And us?"

"I would never think to leave you out. You two will work together to bring death and destruction the world has not seen in thousands of years," Pandora answered. "The humans were so primitive that they did not even have a name for you. With everything we will accomplish, they will never have the chance to name you." She chuckled.

Two creatures stood before her with elongated necks and leopard bodies. Their heads swayed back and forth as their tails twitched in anticipation. "We will leave nothing behind." They looked at each other.

"We will feast on their fear and fuel our bodies with their blood. They will search the heavens for help and find silence." They flicked their tongues.

Pandora clapped her hands and bounced excitedly. "I knew that I made the correct choice with you. True terror does not need a name. Go friends. Feast!" she yelled.

Chapter 4

"So, let's say we find Ra and he's all for this fight, what do we do then? Are we supposed to trap Pandora, kill her, bury her alive? I'm all for jumping into a fight, prepared or not, but this? I feel way too underprepared to even walk out this door right now," Haydeez said as she paced the room. "Shouldn't we work this out more before we just run off?"

Linx laughed. "Wow. You want to plan? Seriously? I should mark this down somewhere."

Haydeez threw a pillow at him. "Funny. You're just hilarious. We have to be ready for this."

Keeglian cleared his throat. "I could research. There will be something written on this somewhere. I figured out that we need Ra. Surely I'll find out what he will need to stop her as well. However, it does seem odd that we would need an Egyptian god to stop a Greek creation." He paused for a moment, lost in his thoughts.

Haydeez waved her hand in front of his face. "Not really that weird. I mean, think of all the stuff she's let out so far. Celtic, Greek, and apparently now we have Egyptian. I don't think it matters. Evil is evil no matter who believes in it. Why do you think these work?" she asked as she picked up her necklace full of charms, each a different religious symbol and each with its own strength. "Belief is really all you need. Now, each of these is a different belief but underneath it all is basically the same thing. So, maybe some of it crosses over. I mean, look at the Greeks and Romans. Their whole structure is almost exactly the same."

Keeglian nodded. "That is true, I suppose. In that case, I will continue my search for the elusive weapon while you hunt for our god. I will contact you with more information once I locate it. Best of luck to you, duckie. You will succeed," he said. He picked up his pile of books and papers and walked back to the bathroom door. He drew a few symbols on the door with his finger and knocked. With a quick nod at Haydeez he opened the door and walked back through to his store.

Haydeez flopped down on the bed and heaved a heavy sigh. "Just hunt for a god. Sounds easy enough to me." She turned over, crawled up to her pillow and buried her face.

Linx smiled. "At least you don't have to do it all alone," he joked. "So, do we start now or try to get some sleep first? To be honest, I'm still up for a movie if you're interested. Something to take my mind off of everything before we start digging into it all. What do you think, love? Movie time?" Linx asked with the remote in hand.

Haydeez peeked out from her pillow. "Ok. You twisted my arm."

●　　　●　　　●

Linx checked the clock. "Hey, kitchen's open." He stretched and reached for the phone. "Let's get some breakfast up here."

"You're just looking for more excuses to avoid starting this search, aren't you?" Haydeez asked with a chuckle. "You do know that we have to find him no matter what, right? If he's the only way to stop her, we need to find him as soon as possible." She sat up and scooted to the end of the bed. "So, where do we start our search?"

"Under my breakfast after I finish eating it," Linx answered. He dialed the kitchen to place his order.

Haydeez waved him off and went to sit at the table. She pulled out a laptop while Linx put in an order. As she opened it, a steady beep sounded. "Crap. What happened now?" As she pulled up the window, she groaned. "Looks like our search will have to wait. What the hell did she let out now?"

"Thanks," Linx said and hung up the phone. "What's happening, love? What did it find now?" he asked. He leaned over her shoulder and read the article. "An earthquake? How is that out of the ordinary? Earthquakes happen all the time."

Haydeez pointed to the screen and said, "True, but they don't last for hours at a time, do they? What the heck causes earthquakes that last that long? And when was the last time you saw an earthquake travel?" She pointed to the locations of the earthquake. "One person said that it felt like the earth rolled under her feet. She said she could see it rolling away from her. Still think it's not one of ours?" She sighed. "Do we follow the same strategy this time? So far, we've dealt with a couple of Egyptian weird things. Do we assume she's letting out Egyptian creatures this time? I mean, she seems to be collecting a lot of energy in this area."

"I wonder if it's because the whole of humanity supposedly came from Africa. You know, that whole 'cradle of life' thing," he said. "Maybe this is a mythological hot spot. Or maybe I don't know what I'm talking about and she's just going to do whatever she wants and we have no idea what's happening."

Haydeez shook her head. "Well, we've flown blind before, so, let's put our blindfolds on and start looking." She started to type. "They would probably hide him in plain sight but we would think it's something different from what's actually there, like that lighthouse. That was so cool. What's the most recognizable thing in Egypt?"

"The desert?" Linx asked. "I mean, the whole country's a bloody desert, right?"

"Pyramids? The sphinx?" Haydeez asked. "When was the last time you checked on Bebo?"

"Yesterday. He ate a shoe. Probably mine, but he hates me. So, I expect it. Your boyfriend's fine too. He misses you and wants to know when you're coming back to go for a ride," he answered.

Haydeez smiled. "I could use one right now. Bike, horse, whatever. It doesn't matter. A ride would clear my head and help me think straight. Don't forget to let her know we'll be staying longer than planned. I'll wire her extra for the inconvenience."

Linx nodded.

There was a knock on the door as her phone rang.

Linx motioned to the door as she answered the call. "Fancy hearing from you, Peter. To what do I owe the pleasure today?" she asked.

"Haydeez, glad I caught you. I hope you're not too busy. I've got a job for you," Peter said. "You're not too busy, right?"

Haydeez threw her head back and rolled her eyes. "Depends on what you're offering and what you want. I'm in the middle of another job right now. Unless it's life or death, it'll have to wait till I'm done here."

"Well, there seems to be a couple of serpopards roaming around Egypt right now. They're killing and destroying everything in their path. I'm sure it can wait, how did you put it, till you're done there? I mean, it's not like life or death or anything," Peter answered.

She sighed. "What the hell is a serpopard? And where in Egypt is it?"

"I'll send you the information and your fee. You let me know when they're destroyed. Simple as that," he said. She could almost hear the smirk as he spoke.

"Of course, Peter. Always a pleasure to work with you and your super-secret friends over there. Looking forward to seeing you soon," she said. "Want to go grab a coffee with me when it's done? Maybe have lunch?"

"Just notify me when it's done, Ms. Blackhawk," Peter answered abruptly.

She smirked. "Right. It's probably best not to date your help. Gives a bad impression. Should we meet in private? Perhaps you could come by my hotel before I head home."

"Good day, Ms. Blackhawk," Peter answered and disconnected the call.

Haydeez laughed. "I love to make him uncomfortable. Take my shots where I can get them. I wish I could see his face when I talk to him. Bet he gets all embarrassed and flustered and all that. He's such a jerk. Unfortunately, we've got something else to go after now. Coincidentally, it's somewhere in Egypt. What are the odds that this is one of hers too?" she asked.

Linx nodded. "Pretty sure you're probably right."

"We just have to wait for the last location, and how much they're paying me," she added with a smile. Seconds after she finished that statement, her phone beeped. "Well, that was quick." She paused, her brow furrowed. "I have no idea what this thing is. I've never heard of anything like this. Listen to this: body of a leopard, long neck and head of a serpent, spits venom, can knock through a wall with a swing of its neck. There's a pair of them. I don't even know where to begin with this thing." She looked up at Linx. "I really hope it's just flesh because I'm completely lost right now. Have you ever heard of a serpopard?"

Linx shook his head. "Is that all he gave you?" he asked.

With a nod, Haydeez said, "Nothing else but a location." She sniffed the air. "Bring that over here. I'm going to look up this thing and see what

I can find." She sat down at the table and began to type. After several minutes, she cocked her head to the side. "This thing pre-dates language. There's no actual name for it. People have just called it a serpopard because that's all they could come up with. There are no hieroglyphics for it or anything. It only shows up in pre-Dynastic and Mesopotamian art." She turned to Linx. "It's from nomad times when people just started to build homes and establish some kind of settlement. I don't know how to kill it. This is literally all there is. Nobody knows what they do, how to destroy them, what they're called. Where the hell did this thing come from?"

"Really, love? Something like this? You have no idea where it could've come from?" Linx asked. "You're not stupid. It's not something that's still around today, so, that means it can die. Since humans became stronger, bolder, and more industrious, obviously, somehow it was killed. We just have to figure out how to do that," he said matter-of-factly.

Haydeez shrugged her shoulders. "We have to figure out how? Is that all? Well, why didn't you just say that to begin with? Seems easy enough. How about you take a stab at that and I'll finish my breakfast?" She handed him the laptop and walked over to the bed with her food. She nodded to the screen. "Tag, you're it," she added and took a bite of a piece of toast.

Linx chuckled. "Ok, since I'm so much better at research than you are, I'll go ahead and 'take a stab' as you put it. Shouldn't be too hard." He set down the laptop and cracked his knuckles. "Hey, what about your iron dagger? Will that work?"

Haydeez shook her head. "Nope, only works for mystical things: the siren, witches, kelpies, stuff like that. They have that magic aura around them. The iron dampens it." She took another bite and stopped. "Wait. The dagger," she said with a mouth full of food. Her eyes grew wide. With her food still in hand she jumped up and searched for her phone. "There it is. I need to call Piven," she mumbled around the food. With a grunt, she swallowed and dialed. "Please be there, please be there. Oh! Hey, it's Haydeez. I have a really super important question to ask you. I need to use your dagger. Wait, that's not a question. Can I use your dagger? May I use your dagger?"

Cornelius chuckled. "Good evening to you Ms. Blackhawk. I hope you're doing well. I assume you're referring to the beniice dagger in the glass case downstairs. The one that's supposed to change the seasons. Can I ask why you will need it, dear?"

Haydeez took a deep breath. "So sorry to be rude. That totally wasn't my intention. I'm fine. We're in the middle of a hunt right now and we're trying to figure out a way to stop this thing that's older than civilization. I'm going to guess that modern tools will not work. But what if the weather can kill it? What do you think?"

"I think you may be smarter than you give yourself credit for, dear. I would say that idea makes sense. One can only use the tools available and if you don't have any more information from civilized eras, I would say that this thing was no longer around by that point. So, it stands to reason that something killed it. So, when do you need this dagger?" he asked.

With a sigh, she answered, "Now. Well, within the next couple hours probably. I'm hunting it as we speak."

"Hmm, well, where are you? I will do my best to get it to you quickly," Cornelius responded.

Haydeez chuckled. "Well, that's the thing. We're kind of in Egypt at the moment. That's where it is. If I had known about it before now, I would've said something before we left the country but I just found out about it maybe an hour ago. I don't expect you to just hop a plane and come out here or anything. I sort of had another plan."

"You're going to ask Keeglian, aren't you?" Linx blurted out.

Haydeez nodded. "I have a friend that can come get it from you and bring it here quickly," she added.

"Well, dear, unless your friend can transport himself in the blink of an eye, I would say it's probably going to be a while," Cornelius said.

"That's the thing. He can," Haydeez said.

Linx sighed. "I'll get him on the phone now." He dialed the number and waited.

There was silence on the line as Cornelius tried to comprehend the information he had just been given. Finally, he said, "Well, I would say that sounds quite interesting and I would love to see that in action." He chuckled. "I learn more every time I speak to you. There is more in this world that I don't understand than what I do, but I must thank you for opening my eyes and allowing me to acquire this knowledge."

"Well, we help each other," Haydeez answered. "You have been more help to me recently than I could've asked for and I appreciate it greatly. I really don't know if I would've come up with this without seeing your dagger first." She turned to Linx who gave her a quick smile. "Ok, so he said he'll come get it from you and bring it here to us. I need you to get to a door."

Chapter 5

A knock sounded on the bathroom door again. When Haydeez opened it, Keeglian stood with Cornelius Piven at his back. Cornelius stood with his eyes wide and head cocked to the side. She motioned the men inside. He took a tentative step and poked his head past the threshold.

"This is probably the most bizarre thing I have ever seen and I just had a gorgon steal an egg from my home," Cornelius said. He moved slowly into the room. "Greetings, Ms. Blackhawk. Mr. Linx, it's a pleasure to meet you in person finally." He reached out to shake hands with Linx. "May I?" he asked as he motioned to the closed curtains. A slight gasp escaped his lips as he pulled the curtains open. "Remarkable," he mumbled. "Positively amazing."

Haydeez smiled. "Welcome to Egypt, Mr. Piven." She turned to Keeglian and added, "Thanks for bringing him here. That's one problem solved. Any luck yet on the other issues?"

"Once we find him and release him, we will need to get him back to where he belongs and that will prove difficult without his ship. He flies his ship across the heavens to bring the sunrise every morning, or so the stories tell. Whether he actually supplies the sunrise or not does not matter. He will still need to be returned to his place," Keeglian explained. "I would suggest that you hunt and we stay here to search for his ship. It's best to split resources when on a time crunch." He pulled a watch out of a small pocket on his vest and checked the time. "The shop is closed, so I do not need to worry about anything back at home. I'm free to assist you here for now." He tucked the watch back into the pocket and tugged his vest smooth. "Does that sound agreeable?" he asked.

With a nod, Haydeez answered, "Sure, but it's going to have to wait until after I take care of the other issue. I needed that dagger to take care of the 'serpopards' that Peter called me about. Conveniently, they're right here in Egypt, so I don't need to do a lot of extra travelling. I hate packing and unpacking, over and over.

"Oh yes, the dagger. Of course," Cornelius turned from the window and closed the curtains. "Yes, here it is." He pulled a thin box from the inside of his coat and handed it to Haydeez. "Please be sure to recite the incantation correctly. You don't want to make a mistake with that. I would hate to see you strike yourself down instead of these creatures. That would certainly put a damper on things," he said with a chuckle.

Haydeez opened the box and ran her fingers over the dagger. The magic inside sang to her. It sounded like raindrops against a tin roof. She breathed in and the scent of a fresh rainfall tickled her nostrils. Goosebumps marched up the backs of her arms and made the hair on her neck stand up. She could see something in the silver and gold veins move. At first she thought it was just the way the light played off the metal but the more she looked, the more movement she saw. Her breath caught in her throat and a gasp passed her parted lips. "Lightning," she whispered. "So much lightning. It's beautiful." Her body shuddered and she pulled her fingers back. She shook her head and closed the box. As she looked around the room, everyone looked back at her, confusion and concern in their eyes.

"Are you alright, love?" Linx asked. He stood away from her with his brow furrowed.

"Yea, I'm fine. Why?" she asked.

Keeglian pointed to her face. "You were not your cheerful self for a moment, duckie. I mean, you were you, but your face..." He paused for a moment as he tried to find the words. He turned to face Cornelius. "What exactly do you know about this dagger, sir?"

Cornelius shook his head. "You know as much as I do at this point. I have only learned that it was used by a shaman to bring about the change in seasons thousands of years ago. It can bring lightning and storms as needed. It just depends on the incantation you recite. Beyond that, this is all new to me. I've often questioned the validity of many of my pieces until Ms. Blackhawk came along. She has been able to confirm at least a few of my items are the real deal. While I don't know exactly what it does, I know that it has true power in there."

"That doesn't explain what just happened to her though," Linx interrupted. "Does anyone know what that was?"

Haydeez waved her hands around. "Excuse me. What are you talking about? What happened to me? Why is everyone looking at me funny?" she asked.

"Your eyes changed and your hair started to move, kind of like it does when a breeze is blowing," Linx answered. "You lost yourself for a moment. I don't know where you went, but you weren't here in this room anymore. Well, your body was, but your mind went somewhere else entirely. It was eerie."

Cornelius ran a hand through his hair. "I wonder if you were channeling a past shaman. Do you have magic blood? Are there witches in your family?" he asked.

Haydeez shook her head. "No idea. Joseph took me in when I was a baby. I have no idea who my parents were or if anyone in my family ever did magic. I wish I did because maybe that would explain why everyone keeps calling me a mutt and telling me my blood is muddy," she said. "It's getting to be very annoying."

Cornelius nodded. "Hmm. That's possible. Well, no matter. Whatever you have in your blood, that dagger likes you. It seems to have bonded to you already. I've touched it many times and it has never responded to me like that. All I see is a stone dagger but you," he paused and rubbed his chin. "You said you saw lightning inside it. It showed itself to you because it trusts you. I came here to help with your fight, but I'll be leaving here with one less artifact I suppose," he added with a chuckle. "That dagger has a new home now, Ms. Blackhawk."

With her mouth hung open, she just stared at him. Finally, she found her voice again. "I can't take this. It belongs in your collection. It's not right for me to just keep it. I just wanted to borrow it for this job." She shook her head. "No, I can't take it."

Cornelius laughed. "I do not believe that is your choice at this time, Ms. Blackhawk. Consider it a gift, a thank you. When all of this is over, you will come to my home and help me weed out all the fake pieces from the authentic artifacts of power." He turned to Keeglian. "Well, since I don't need to wait around anymore for the dagger to return, I can help you research. Where do we start?"

Chapter 6

Sobek slipped through the darkness with ease. He managed to blend into everything in spite of his size and the large sun disc that sat atop his head. His scales glistened with their own inner glow in the shadows. The massive creature moved slowly but with a purpose. The lights ahead were bright and called to him. The lights laughed at him, mocked him. He eyed the buildings with disgust. "My worshipers would never demean themselves with such outlandish structures. These abominations to our ways should be destroyed," he growled and snapped his jaws. "How are they to be one with the Nile when they seat themselves so far off the ground? Pitiful humans. They do not understand what they have done."

His eyes rolled back into his head and he whispered to himself. The disc on top of his head began to glow. He repeated the same words continuously. The light grew brighter until it lit the entire area in sunlight. Then, the light shot straight out from the disc and hit the building. A fiery hole formed in the structure. Sobek dragged the beam across the building like a knife and sliced it in half.

The ground began to shake and part of the building slid off. Bricks and metal beams crashed down into the sands. Clouds of dust and debris flew up into the air. Screams could be heard amidst the veil.

"Perhaps you will learn from your mistakes, humans. You must stay within reach of the life-giving Nile instead of trying to reach for Ra. You are not meant to walk in the heavens with Ra," Sobek said. "There is still a chance for some of you to make amends, those of you who have not already died."

He threw his head back and whispered. An intense white light burned in the disc. His eyes opened and the beam shot from the disc again. It sliced through another building with ease. Fires blazed as the second building crumbled into the ground.

Sobek casually watched, proud of his work. He walked slowly and scanned the damage. His anger mirrored in the carnage he had caused.

Screams could be heard. People shouted, begged for help. The chorus of panic radiated to the outer edges of the cloud of rubble. Voices pleaded for someone to explain what had happened, why it happened.

Sobek watched. "These are not dangers of the Nile. You have displeased your god and now you must be punished. How does it feel to displease me, humans? Perhaps others will learn from your mistakes. You will serve as an example to them." He stood with his hands locked behind his back. A smug smile spread across his jaws. "You will bow before me again, as you should. I am your god. Nobody else will protect you!"

The people could not hear him over their own screams. Bodies writhed on the ground. Blood sizzled in the flames.

Sobek stood on the banks of the Nile. He knelt down and dipped his fingers into the water. "I protected you from what lurks beneath the surface, what trudges through the muck down below. What has happened to this land that caused you all to forget what we have done for you?" He bent further down and dipped his open mouth into the water to take a drink. When he stood back up, it dripped from his pointed teeth. "You have all become a danger to yourselves. I must now protect you," he paused and looked around once more. "From you."

Chapter 7

"We have another problem," Haydeez said. "How are we going to explain this away? I mean, these creatures are terrorizing people. I'm sure it's been caught on camera by now. How do we explain this? Or do we just let it go? Do we bother trying to explain it or just let it be another Loch Ness Monster? I can set off one of Linx's little bugs to stop anything from being recorded while I'm taking it down but what about anything that's already happened?" she asked.

They all looked at each other. "Hadn't thought that far ahead, dear," Cornelius answered. "Is that even your job? Why does it matter if people know what's out there?"

Haydeez cocked her head to the side and furrowed her brow. "I don't know. I guess I just always assumed that it wasn't allowed, that we couldn't let people know about this stuff. It's something that you see in the movies all the time and stuff. When people find out, they freak out." She said. "If we're not keeping everything a secret, then why am I pushing people away? Why do I have to hide what I do? Why is there a secret organization watching us from a few doors down in this hotel? I know you guys are down there. I saw you pull up," she said as she turned to the door.

A knock sounded on the door.

"Oh come on," Linx yelled.

Haydeez walked to the door and opened it. "Yup. I'm still *that* good," she said. "Can we help you? Make it quick. We're a little busy discussing how to save the world and all that."

Without an invitation, Agent Blue and Agent Red walked into the hotel room. "Cozy," Agent Blue said. "Since we're all being besties, I figured we should probably share a little tidbit of information with you." She looked around the room. "Interesting company you choose to keep, Ms.

Blackhawk. Are you certain they can be trusted?" she asked. She scrunched her nose and glared at each of the men in turn.

"Speak your piece and leave. The only ones I don't completely trust are the ones who just got here. In case you're wondering, that would be you," Haydeez answered. "I thought we were done with all this animosity and posturing. I'm sure that you're number one where you come from, but when you happen to be on my turf, I'm the alpha dog. You keep trying to mark my trees and I'm going to attack. So, either you're here to share information or you're here to insult my company. One of those ends in a fight."

Agent Blue smiled. "Wouldn't dream of insulting your little friends, Ms. Blackhawk." She motioned for Agent Red to close the door and stand against it. When the room was once again secured, she added. "Now, that bit of information I was talking about. It seems that your little friend has possibly brought another of her special buddies out of that little box of hers."

Haydeez scoffed. "And why would you think it's one of hers?"

"Because it just took out two buildings along the Nile with a laser mounted on the top of its head," Agent Red blurted from the door.

"As crazy as that sounds, I still don't see how that makes it one of hers," Haydeez answered. "Do you know what did it? What does it look like? Wait..." she turned to face Agent Red. "Did you just say the buildings were on the Nile? So, whatever it is just happens to be right here, right where we are now? Does anyone else find that weird?" she asked. "That's the fourth thing that's been right here in Egypt. That means she's got to be building up her strength here. But now I'm really confused. Pandora is Greek. Why is she powering up here in Egypt? Does anyone else understand this at all?"

Everyone shook their heads.

"Do you think that means she's trying to bring her kids here to kill them?" Linx asked. "She can't do that, can she? I thought the egg was supposed to bring them back to where they were first born and they die together."

Cornelius stood. "I suppose it doesn't matter where they are called to as long as they die in the place of their first birth. We can only assume that she is building up her base here and then she will have to return to that location."

"Unless she plans on just killing them," Agent Red said. "Wouldn't that stop the world if they both just died?" he asked with his arms crossed.

"Crap," Haydeez blurted. "She's going to build up her power here and then just kill them. It doesn't matter if they make it back to their first birth place. She can kill them anywhere."

Cornelius shook his head. "I don't believe that they can die anywhere else. Otherwise, a car accident, stray bullet, cancer, something would take them before their time. I think we're safe to assume that she will still need to take them back to kill them. But she still needs to gain power in order to do it. So, right now, we still need to destroy whatever it is that she has been letting out." He locked his hands together behind his back. "Unfortunately, that means we're just helping her along in her venture."

Agent Blue turned to face Haydeez. "So, are we just going to ignore the fact that something is out there shooting lasers from its head that can slice a building in half and collapse it in seconds? I don't care who's funding it. It's my job to kill it," she said. "I hope you understand what I'm saying because I'm not going to just sit by and wait for you to take care of this one. I'm only here to share information and then we're going to go after it ourselves. Do whatever you need to do but I'm not going to let this thing rip apart another city." She handed Haydeez a piece of paper. "If you plan to join the fun, this is where we'll be," she added and moved to the door.

Agent Red opened the door and the two agents left without another word.

"Well, they are certainly vibrant and chatty," Keeglian said.

Everyone jumped at the sound of his voice. "Bloody hell, forgot you were even here, mate. Did you hide yourself or something?" Linx asked. He shook his head. "So, what are we doing now?" He sighed heavily. "We have to find Ra and release him from whatever it is that's holding him, we have to kill these pre-civilization creatures that shoot venom and knock over buildings with their crazy strong necks, and now we have to go after something that shoots lasers from a thing mounted on its head. Does that cover everything? It probably doesn't but hey, for now I think it does." He threw his hands up in the air. "What's next?"

"Never ask that," Haydeez responded immediately. "It's just going to invite something worse. Haven't you ever watched a movie? You're taunting the bad guy." She shook her head and scoffed.

"What is wrong with you?" Linx asked.

Haydeez sighed. "That's a story for another day. So, let's go make sure we have another day. Get to work on Ra's location and I'll go take care of the serpopard. If they want to go after the other thing on their own, that's their choice. They didn't even ask what we had going on or why we were here. I can't allow our target to run around and keep killing. They can't let theirs do the same. I'm only one person. Can't do both."

Cornelius stepped towards Haydeez. "Do be careful. I don't believe that we will be able to do this without all of us being here. That includes you, Ms. Blackhawk." He took her hand. "Aim for the heart. Never cut off the head just in case it's like one of those hydra things. Remember that we know nothing about this one. There is no history on it." He picked up the box and handed it to her again. "Let it guide you. You'll know what to do. It will show you everything you need to know. It appears to be a sentient dagger," he whispered. "You will be successful."

She took the box with a smile. "I'm going to enjoy this."

Chapter 8

Haydeez picked up her phone and groaned. "Yes, Peter, I'm in the process of hunting it down and killing it as we speak. I do hope that this is important because I'm a little busy right now." She pulled her rental off the road and parked next to the remains of a building. There was still dust in the air. "This one's new," she mumbled.

Peter cleared his throat. "We seem to have another problem. Those serpopards are not the only thing out there destroying buildings and killing people. There's something out there sucking the souls out of people. It's just leaving a dried out body behind. For some reason, it also seems to be in your area. Is there something happening that we need to be aware of?" he asked.

"If you feel like you need to know, then perhaps you should find out. I don't provide you with the local news. You tell me what to kill, you pay me, and then our business is done. You're supposed to be the one with all the information, Peter. Remember?" she answered with venom in her words. "Just send me what you have on this other thing and I'll get to it when I get to it. Obviously, I'm still working on the other problem I need to solve for you. Is there anything else I can do for you today, Peter? Would you like me to pick up your dry cleaning or wax your car too? No? Then I really need to get back to this. Seems like it's going to be a long day." She ended the call before he had the chance to say anything else. "I really hate you, Peter," she added after the call disconnected.

She shook the phone and growled. With a sigh, she then dialed Linx. "Hey, we've got another problem. It looks like everything is happening now."

"What do you mean 'everything'?" he asked tentatively.

"My BFF called again. There's another thing out there. He said it's sucking the souls out of people and leaving just an empty, dried up body," she answered. "Any idea what that could be?"

Linx groaned. "Stealing souls? Hmm... We're in Egypt." He paused. Only the click of keys could be heard on the other end. "So, in Egyptian mythology, the only thing that has to do with souls is the creature from the afterlife that devours your soul during judgement. Basically, when you die, your soul is judged. If it is found wanting, then Ammit will devour it to torture you for eternity. Sounds like it's a neutral creature. If this is out there, it shouldn't be killing everyone. It should only be going after evil, right?"

Haydeez shrugged. "I have no idea. Maybe it's confused because these are living people instead of dead spirits. Wait, if this is a soul eater, how am I supposed to kill it? It's supposed to be there for all eternity, eating souls and judging people, right? So, how do we stop it from killing everyone?"

"Ms. Blackhawk, this is Cornelius. I think maybe it's possible to stop this thing and destroy it. From what you've told me, Pandora needs to gain power for her plan to work. In order to gain power, she's letting things out of the box," Cornelius started. "So, she's letting it out to be killed because she can't pull their energy directly from the disc, right? That tells me that she wants you to kill it, which means there has to be a way to kill it. She wouldn't let it out if there was no way for her to gain its power."

Haydeez paused for a minute. Her eyes moved across the broken pieces of building, lost in thought. "What if only the power of a god could kill these things?" she mumbled. "What if this thing is what we need to get rid of all of them?" She ran her fingers over the box with the beniice dagger tucked safely inside. "After everything we've already done, we just run into this one hoping it will work? Could this actually work?" she asked.

"Either way we end up in the same place. Either Pandora gets her power after you kill whatever is out there, or she gets what she wants because you can't kill it and it kills everyone in its path," Linx answered. "The only difference is whether or not you try. Are you ready to jump out there without a safety net, love?"

Haydeez smiled to herself. "Not the first time I've done that I suppose." She grabbed the wooden box and her bag. "Time to mix a little modern with the ancients. I'll call you when it's all done," she said as she ended the call. She took a deep breath and opened the door.

The smell of smoke filled every gasp. Her body froze as she remembered the scene in Boston just a couple short months ago. She could not smell burnt flesh this time but the fires ensured she could still see the devastation. Everywhere she looked was another reminder of an entire city of people that she was not able to save. This time around it was not hollowed out buildings with fires behind the broken windows. It was piles of broken bricks, twisted metal, melted supports. Here the buildings buried the victims alive, choked off their last breaths. What she saw may have been different but the end result was still the same and the urgency was real.

"Here we go again," she whispered to herself. She marked her path like she had done before, with things that stood out in all the destruction. She had to make a conscious effort to steady her breath. Images of Boston flooded her brain and confused her. "This is different. This will end different. I have to believe that," she whispered to herself. "Linx would tell me to push forward, that I can't save everyone, but the ones I save will be forever grateful."

The ground shook and screams filled the air. A cloud of dirt, dust, and broken bricks puffed between two buildings.

Haydeez ran straight into the debris. She rounded the corner and stood frozen as her eyes adjusted. Her heart thumped in her chest as the ground finally settled. Two figures stood with their backs to Haydeez. She was not sure if she expected them to be bigger because everything else she had faced so far was oversized in some way or maybe because she had built them up so much in her brain from what little information they had. "They were supposed to be some kind of ancient thing that was so old it did not even have a name. Shouldn't they be god-like and gigantic or something," she mumbled to herself. Her mind just told her that they should be larger for some reason. "Doesn't matter though. I still have to kill you both."

With her body in the shadows, she pulled out a familiar little gadget and checked her watch. "Alright, 20 minutes to deal with this thing. Let's hope this works." She pressed the button and added, "Starting now." She dropped the device and pulled the dagger from the box. Under the top was a short inscription. She read the words aloud slowly to ensure they were correct. The dagger pulsed in her hand. It hummed and sang to her as if to welcome her to its world. Her fingers closed gently around the dagger. After she spoke the last words, she whispered, "Thank you."

With her eyes on the creatures, she raced from the shadows and screamed, "Time's up!"

The serpopards turned and watched as the human ran straight at them with nothing but a shiny little dagger. They looked at each other. The sound that came from their mouths was a mixture of a gurgle and a laugh. They stood for a moment as she made her way towards them.

Without any warning, Haydeez stopped. Her eyes turned black and flickers of light sparked within the depths of the darkness.

The creatures paused, confusion apparent on their serpentine faces. They both took a tentative step towards Haydeez.

"Step into my parlor said the spider to the fly," Haydeez whispered. "It's the prettiest little parlor that you ever did spy." She smirked.

Behind the creatures, clouds had begun to gather and roll. Lightning flashed within the clouds and thunder rumbled the skies.

"Step a little closer and you'll see my pretty little web." She swiped the dagger through the air in front of her body. Lightning crackled and ripped through the sky. It twisted and arced in a web-like pattern from the clouds down to the ground.

Thunder boomed and the lightning struck one of the creatures. Fur, flesh, and scales sprayed everywhere. The smell of cooked meat filled the air and mixed with the smoke and debris. The creature did not have time to scream because the strike hit faster than it could anticipate. It was now a heap of charred flesh on the ground. The body twitched as the last bits of life escaped through the gaping hole in the creature's body.

The second creature shrieked and turned towards Haydeez. Anger burst from its eyes as it inhaled deeply. When it released the breath, it shot a glob of greenish goop from its mouth.

Haydeez spun out of the way with ease. Her black eyes turned back to the creature. Large sparks exploded from her eyes and arced up around her face. "That will not work," she said flatly. "You will die now." She turned around and threw her head back.

The creature did not wait for her to attack this time. After it saw what happened to the other serpopard, it reared back its snake head and prepared to strike her.

When it snapped its head at her, Haydeez spun around and slammed the dagger into the side of the creature's head. Lightning pulsed from the dagger into the creature. It screamed in agony as the power flowed throughout its entire body. It convulsed violently but Haydeez just stood with her hand fixed on the dagger. She watched as smoke rose from the creature's body and cooked it from the inside. "I told you that you will die now," she said calmly.

By the time the second creature dropped to the ground, the first had already shriveled. All that was left was a badly burned, unrecognizable corpse. Had she tried to look for it, Pandora's symbol would have been almost impossible to find.

But she did not. Haydeez just turned from the bodies and began to walk back the way she had come. Lightning still flashed in her eyes. Blood dripped from the dagger as she held it tight in her hand. Without a glance or a thought, she bent down, scooped up her bag and Linx's device, and continued to walk back to the car. Her rigid movements appeared forced, as if something else had control of her body.

When she reached the car, she quickly climbed inside and dropped her bag on the floor. Then, everything went black.

Chapter 9

"Haydeez! Answer me!" Linx yelled. "What the hell is going on?" He slammed his fist on the table and stood up. "I need to go find her," he said and moved toward the door.

Keeglian cleared his throat and said, "That would be unwise. She will answer. And if she does not, what do you intend to do? Kill the thing that she could not kill? Are you a better fighter, a more skilled assassin? I have seen her work long enough to know she will answer. She always answers." He clasped his hands behind his back.

Linx clenched his fists and growled. He threw his hands up in the air and walked into the bathroom. The door slammed.

Cornelius cocked his head to the side and said, "Oh, well that explains this whole situation." He waved his hand back and forth between the two beds. "How long have they been together?" he asked.

Keeglian shook his head. "They are not, Mr. Piven. It is none of my business but human courting rituals are completely ridiculous. I never understood them. When these situations come up, I try to ignore them. It all just seems too messy to me."

There was a yell from the bathroom followed by a thump.

"Should we check on him?" Cornelius asked.

"Does not seem necessary," Keeglian answered.

Cornelius shook his head and chuckled. "It never gets easier, kid," he mumbled.

Both men turned to look at the computer together as a beep pulsed slowly. The bathroom door flew open and Linx stood in the doorway.

"What is that?" he asked. He cleared the distance between the door and the table in a couple large strides. "Haydeez? Can you hear me?" Linx asked the computer.

All he heard in response was a groan.

Linx heaved a heavy sigh. "I can hear you. Can you speak?" he asked. "Are you alright?"

A muffled voice answered. There were not any clear words, just noises.

"Haydeez, I can't understand you. Are you alright?" Linx yelled. Panic had set in and he began to shake. He stared blankly at the screen as he hoped for something to give him some kind of clue where she was and whether or not she was hurt. "Don't do this again, love," he whispered. His foot tapped rapidly and he ran his hand through his hair.

Cornelius placed a hand on Linx's shoulder. "How is she communicating with you right now, son? Could there be a problem with the line?"

Linx shook his head quickly. "It's meant to work like a 2-way radio but without the need for one of those buttons. It works on a different frequency than regular radio or cell phone communications. I made it for situations like this," he said as he waved a hand at the screen. "But for whatever reason I can't understand her. She could be out there somewhere with her throat ripped out, bleeding to death and I'm just sitting here doing what? Nothing! I'm doing nothing to bloody help!" He stood up and knocked the chair to the floor. "Damn it!" he yelled and started to pace.

"What are you yelling about?" a familiar voice asked from the computer. "I can hear you just fine," Haydeez said, her voice scratchy. She sounded as if she just woke up and could use another four hours sleep.

Linx tripped over the chair as he turned around. "Haydeez! Love, what the hell happened? Are you alright? Where are you? Do you need help?" He blurted out questions faster than she had the chance to answer.

Haydeez groaned. "Slow down. I feel like someone is sitting on my head right now," she answered, her voice was soft. "Please don't talk so loud. You're echoing in my head, like I'm in a cave or something. It feels so weird. I really don't like this at all." She groaned again.

Linx took a deep breath and let it out slowly. "Are you somewhere safe? Are you hurt?" he asked, his voice just above a whisper.

"Yeah, I'm in the car. Other than this train doing laps in my brain right now, I'm fine," she answered. "It'll probably take me a bit to get back there. I don't think I can drive right now, at least not until I can see straight."

Linx threw his head back and closed his eyes as he tried to process what she said. "So, you're not hurt. I'd say that's a win. What about the leopard, snake, things? Where are they?" he asked.

There was a bump and scrape sound. "Oh I totally killed them," she paused. "I think. I think that was me. I'm pretty sure I did it. Ok, so let's just put it this way. They're no longer alive. I can call Peter and let him know it's done, although I don't have a picture because I don't think it was me that walked away. It was all really weird and fuzzy. I have no idea how I got back here. I think I may have blacked out at some point. No, I'm sure I blacked out because I woke up with my face in the floorboard."

Linx cocked his head to the side. "I'm sorry. What? You woke up with your face in the floorboard? Did you hit your head on something?"

"Ugh, I have no idea. Like I said, I don't really know how I got back here," she answered. "Maybe everything will come back to me after I wake up a little more."

"Can we go back to the part where you're not sure if it was you that killed those things? What do you mean by that? Who else could've done it?" Linx asked. He picked up the chair and sat again. "None of this is making any sense. I can come out and get you if you need me to."

Haydeez cleared her throat. "No, I'll be fine. Just give me a little bit. There's nobody here right now. I don't have to worry about anyone touching my body. Those things pretty much took down the buildings. Thankfully, there weren't too many people around but there were still casualties." She sighed. "I could hear them screaming. It was like Boston all over again. I need to stop this. So many people keep dying while I'm right there and I can't stop them. Why can't I stop them?" she groaned. "Wow. That hurts. Ok, so I need to end this now. This can't keep going."

Linx answered, "Just get back here and we'll figure it all out, love. Be safe."

Linx jumped as the lock clicked and the door opened. He ran to the door. "So glad you're back, love. Are you feeling better?" He took her arm and walked her into the room.

"I'm not fragile, Linx. Relax. I'm actually much better now," she answered with a smile. "I'm starting to remember little bits and pieces too. Apparently it actually was me that took those things out. By the way, totally called a lightning bolt that fried one of them. Looked like a hot dog that had dropped into a fire. Pretty cool, huh?" she added.

Cornelius raised an eyebrow. "Impressive. Kudos to you, Ms. Blackhawk. I'm thoroughly impressed with your skills. You truly are amazing," he said with a small clap.

Haydeez took a bow and laughed. "I don't know what we would've done if you hadn't already owned the piece we needed."

"Well, there's no telling. To be honest, there were probably plenty of other things out there that could've killed them," Cornelius answered with a shrug. "We just happened to get lucky this time."

Keeglian nodded. "Indeed. Well, I am certainly pleased that you have been successful. I knew that you would return victorious," he said as he took her hand. "Well done, duckie."

Haydeez smiled. "It was really awesome. I have to think really hard about what actually happened, but when I can get my brain to focus, I can see it." Her brow furrowed. "The problem I'm having is that I don't understand what happened after. It was surreal. I could see where I was going but it was like someone else was in the driver's seat. That's truly the only way I can explain it." She sat on the edge of the bed. "I've never had that happen before."

"Did you hear voices?" Cornelius asked. "During the time that you couldn't recall initially, were there voices in your head at the time? I only ask because I'm concerned about your connection to that dagger. You bonded to it instantly. I've held it many times and it has never done to me what it did to you. You seem to be stronger and more receptive to those types of items. Have you had an experience like that before where an item has spoken to you or gotten inside your head?" he asked.

Haydeez looked at everyone. "Define 'spoke to'," she answered. "I mean, they don't talk to me like we're talking right now or anything but sure. I've had other things call to me in the past. The arrow, that one called me." She looked down at her hands. "Also, most of your items have a voice too. I can't really communicate with them. They don't have a brain or anything but it's like this song. I can usually tell by the song what it can do." She looked up and everyone just stared at her, eyes wide. "Um, ok, so... like the arrow had this booming song. It sounds like hooves beating the ground and wings flapping. But it all flowed together."

"And the dagger?" Linx asked tentatively.

Haydeez stood up. "It sounds like rain. Sometimes it's a quiet shower, sometimes it's a thundering storm, but it's there," she answered. "I'm not going crazy. I was right, wasn't I? The dagger worked." She walked over to the closet area and pulled out her coat. "And now this room is getting crowded. I need some air."

Keeglian put his hand up to block Linx. He shook his head as the door closed. "Let her go. She lost herself and that's not something she can handle. For now, let her get some air and clear her head. She'll be fine. This whole ordeal has taken its toll on her and she needs to regain herself."

Cornelius nodded. "She truly has an amazing gift. I would love to learn more about her. There must be something incredible in her past," he mumbled.

"Incredible. Sure. What's more incredible? The part where she was abandoned when she was a newborn. Or maybe the part where she was raised by a total stranger to fight creatures and save the world, not by choice of course," Linx answered. "She's strong because she was forced to be that way. None of this was ever what she wanted. Unfortunately, it keeps pulling her back no matter how hard she tries to get away, and she's tried. Something always brings her back." He ran a hand through his hair again. "And she's just too stubborn to ask for help."

Chapter 10

Pandora breathed in slow and deep. She rolled her head back and forth and felt her muscles stretch. A smile spread across her lips. "That's two down," she whispered. "I knew you would find a way, child. There is always a way."

She stood alone in the middle of the desert. With her arms spread out wide, she felt the life force from the serpopards and welcomed it into her body. It flowed through her like a quiet river in the forest. Her eyes glowed yellow and the disc pulsed in the middle of her chest. She laughed. "You can't win, child. You will continue to aid me and bring about the demise of your precious humans. The end is inevitable." The body that was barely eighteen moments before had now aged by at least three years.

Her eyes shifted back to their original dark brown, almost black. She cocked her head to the side and furrowed her brow. "Well, well, well. Who are they? New players?" She chuckled. "You don't believe you will destroy him, do you? Pathetic humans. Your fate is sealed. Just give up and die. It will be over quicker."

Pandora reached out to all the creatures she released. She watched as they destroyed lives, buildings, property, anything that stood in their ways. While they all had their uses, Pandora enjoyed the more creative ways to torture and kill the humans. "Taking a life is easy. That's why I pulled you out, Apep. You kill and eat your victims. It sends a perfectly clear message. You are there to kill them. However," she paused as she turned her attention to another. "Ammit is so much more diabolical. She drains the souls straight from the bodies and leaves the flesh to writhe in agony as its very essence is ripped away. The pain that the humans must feel when that happens is absolutely delicious." She closed her eyes and threw back her head. "I can feel it ripple over my skin. It's like a fire. I will hate to lose you,

Ammit." She sighed and added, "Your death will be unfortunate but necessary."

Pandora smoothed her hands over her body and examined herself. "My body is almost ready for the final task. I can feel the energy from the others. They will do nicely. They will have more than enough energy to sustain me," she said to herself. "Keep playing my friends. You will draw enough attention to yourselves for her to help you fulfill your destiny." She laughed again. "Silly humans. You are certainly determined to die today. Fighting just prolongs your end."

Chapter 11

A loud bang shook the walls of the hotel room. Everyone turned quickly to the door. Haydeez raced over and checked to see who it was. "What the hell?" she blurted.

"Open it, now," the male voice on the other side shouted urgently.

Haydeez opened the door to let Agent Red into the room. He carried Agent Blue in his arms and placed her gently on the bed.

"What happened to her?" Linx asked.

"Is she going to live?" Agent Red asked. He turned to Haydeez. "You seem to know what's going on. Is she going to live?" he added angrily.

Haydeez shook her head. "I have no idea. What happened?"

Agent Red knelt next to bed and took Agent Blue's hand in his. He whispered something to her in Russian and dropped his forehead onto her hand. When he lifted his head, he said, "That thing we went after... it wasn't alone. We tried to take it down quick but as soon as this other thing showed up, everything changed. I have no idea what it was but it looked like some kind of weird alligator, hippo thing. It squatted down on all fours like a dog or something but when it spoke, it's like it was judging us. The voice was like a high-pitched gravel and it told us both that we deserved to die for the choices we had made. It told us that it would take our souls."

Haydeez looked at Linx. "Ammit. That has to be her. What happened though? How did she end up like this?" Haydeez asked as she motioned to Agent Blue's unconscious body.

"I don't know!" he yelled. "That thing just spoke and then sucked in. That's all I know. When I saw her start to crumble, I threw all my weight into the creature's head and knocked it over. It was enough to break the connection. Then, I just grabbed her and flew away as fast as I could. I don't know what to do. I don't know how to fix this. You need to fix this. You can't let her die!" he yelled again.

"Listen, first of all, you need to calm down. I have no idea what to do about this but I'm sure between all of us, we'll get it all sorted," she answered. "Second, stop yelling at me. That's really not going to get you what want. I warned you guys to stay out of the way because this is beyond your knowledge. You wanted to go out there yourself and then you're surprised when you get hurt. Step back for a minute, take a breath, and stop blaming me for your mistakes." She grabbed him by the shoulder and asked, "Are we good now?"

He jerked out of her grip. "Just fix her," he said through gritted teeth.

"Oh, wow, I get it. You guys are a thing. You don't just work together. You *are* together," Linx said. "Well, I totally get that. I'd be freaked out too if..." he stopped before he finished his sentence.

"If what, Van Martin?" Agent Red asked. His eyes narrowed. "You're just you. You're alone. So how would you understand?" he sneered.

Haydeez stepped between the two of them. "Ok, so before this turns into broken furniture and black eyes, you go over there with her," she said as she motioned for Agent Red to go sit on the bed with Agent Blue. "And you, over here," she added and waved Linx to the other side of the room. "Did you forget your filter today or something?" she whispered. "Why would you say something? This guy is like an active stick of dynamite. Anything will set him off. He's probably just looking for a reason to fight someone right now. Could you please just not say anything for now? Like nothing... at all... No words...please?"

"Nothing at all? Come on. Did you know they were a thing?" Linx asked in a whisper. "I didn't think it would set him off like that. How was I supposed to know?"

Haydeez rubbed her eyes. "You're not supposed to know. But now that you do, just stay quiet. I don't need him raging in our hotel room. We need to figure this out in case the same thing happens when I go after her. If she's sucking the soul out of people, I need to know if I'll survive and if I can reverse it. Ok?"

Linx just nodded in agreement and slid into the corner. He sat quietly on the chair and just watched everyone in the room.

Keeglian walked over to Agent Blue's body. "Would it be alright if I took a look at the young lady? I have a bit of experience with things of this nature. I may be able to help."

Agent Red eyed the strange creature that stood next to him. He nodded once and slid over to make a little room. He lifted her head and rested it on his lap. Her hair covered her eyes as her head shifted. He gently brushed the red strands off her forehead and just watched her. She looked like she was in a restful sleep.

Haydeez felt bad for what had happened. Inside she was angry at them for what they did. They should have waited for her. She was angry that Pandora let this one out. She was angry that all this had started. Most of all, she was angry at herself that she did not stop them first. *I should have said something. I should have told them not to go without me*, she thought to herself. *Why am I blaming myself for their stupidity?* She sighed. "Any ideas, Keeglian? What can we do?" she asked.

"She's still alive, she's breathing. It would appear that she just needs rest. I don't see any permanent damage. It seems that you interrupted Ammit's feast, sir," he said as he looked at Agent Red. "You probably saved her life. I am going to go back to my shop for a few things. Keep her comfortable and warm. Do not let her body temperature drop or she may slip into a coma." He stood up and moved toward the bathroom door. "I will return shortly," he added. With a few knocks and swipes with his finger, he opened the door and stepped inside.

Agent Red's eyes narrowed. "His shop is in the bathroom?" he asked sarcastically.

"Not exactly. It's hard to explain," Haydeez answered. "Don't worry about him. Just make sure you follow his directions completely. I have to make a phone call. I'll be right back." She opened the bathroom door and stepped inside.

He looked at Cornelius and asked, "Is that some kind of portal to another world or something? Everyone goes into the bathroom to leave?"

Cornelius nodded. "That's about right, I suppose. Well, while they're gone why don't we get her situated properly. Mr. Linx, would you be a gentleman and head down to the front desk for some extra blankets? We will need to make sure we wrap her completely."

Linx nodded and walked towards the door and said, "Be right back, mate."

• • •

Linx opened the door to his hotel room and walked inside. He held a stack of three blankets. "Oh come on!" he blurted.

Haydeez sat on her bed with her laptop. She looked up at Linx and smiled. "You got some extra blankets. Cool. We'll need to wrap the two of them to keep their body heat trapped," she said.

Agent Red had propped himself up on the pillows from the other bed. He cradled Agent Blue's body in his lap against his bare chest.

"Please tell me you're still wearing pants, mate," Linx said. "I have to sleep there tonight." He walked over and dropped the blankets on the bed. On the floor next to his bed were Agent Blue's clothes as well as Agent Red's pants. "I hate you, mate." He sighed. "At least I only see trousers here, no boxers."

Agent Red looked him in the eyes and said, "I don't wear any." He pulled her close to him and settled into the bed. His chest muscles flexed as he tightened his grip. His wings folded silently behind his back. They somehow managed to curve down his back to allow him to be comfortable.

Linx looked at Haydeez and motioned to his bed. Haydeez just chuckled and went back to the laptop. Linx scoffed and shook his head. He walked over to the table and sat.

Cornelius took a blanket and chuckled. "Let me get that for you," he said as he moved to wrap the agent. "How would you like me to maneuver around those?" he asked and motioned to the agent's metallic wings.

"They'll move for you. They fold up when needed," he answered. He pulled the blanket up around his girlfriend and tucked it in. He whispered in her ear and nuzzled up to her neck so his warm breath would touch her skin. They sat in silence.

"Did Keeglian get back yet?" Linx asked Haydeez.

She shook her head. "Not yet, but I have some ideas on where to find Ra. Come sit," she said as she patted the bed next to her.

Linx blushed and walked towards her. He sat down on the edge of the bed and leaned just enough to see the screen.

Haydeez raised an eyebrow. "Do I stink or something? Get over here." She grabbed his arm and dragged him onto the bed. "Ok, so last time we did this, we had to find all those pieces, right? But every prison is going to be different. It's going to be based on the prisoner. So, Ra, being the sun god and all, they would probably want to keep him somewhere that he can't see the sun, or at least very little of the sun." She turned the laptop to face Linx completely. "The Great Pyramid of Giza," she said triumphantly.

He looked at the screen and cocked his head to the side. "Ok, so it's big enough and right out in the open. Makes sense but it's completely empty. Where would they keep him?" he asked.

She pointed to a diagram of the pyramid. "The King's Chamber. Look at these open shafts that just open up to the outside. He would be able to see the sun for moments a day, not nearly enough for the god of the sun. It would be an eternity of torture. Think about it. For some reason this entire pyramid was bare when they first excavated it. Nobody knows why those shafts are there. Nobody knows anything about this one. There are too many mysteries for this to be a coincidence. And look at this," she added and pointed to a news story. "There were strange red markings inside a small tunnel, too small for a person to view. They had to send a tiny camera in to explore. What if those markings are the spell that's hiding his prison?" she asked excitedly.

Linx raised his eyebrows. "Well, that actually sounds pretty plausible. We can always go take a look, see if we can get our own equipment in there to check out the markings," he said. "It'll get me away from the naked birdman in my bed. I'm in."

"Hey, Agent Red Eagle, we're stepping out for a little bit. Will you be alright here with Cornelius?" Haydeez asked.

"I think I prefer his company to yours. He tends to stay quiet," he answered.

Haydeez nodded in agreement. "That's true. No arguments here. Well alright then." She turned to Linx. "Ready to go?" she asked with a smile.

•   •   •

"So, what should we tell them?" Linx asked. "I mean, security has been beefed up with all the attacks everywhere. They'll definitely have someone out there. What do you want to tell them?"

Haydeez watched the road. "We should tell them that we're there to see if the pyramid is a prison for one of the ancient gods and see what they say," she chuckled. "I wonder what would happen if we actually told the truth. They'd probably throw us in jail."

"We'd be better off trying to sneak by them," Linx answered. "Besides, I don't think I would make it in jail. I'm a little too pretty. I don't like the idea of being passed around."

"That's true. You definitely wouldn't last," Haydeez joked. "Ok, so, I suggest we use the CDC badge again and tell them we received information that there were people leaving here with an unknown illness. That'll make everyone stay pretty far away while we work."

Linx nodded. "Sounds good. I'm glad it's nighttime. If it was during peak hours right now, it would be hell to get all those tourists out of here. This way we only have to deal with those security folks," he said. With a nod ahead he added, "Let's see if it works."

•   •   •

"I can't believe you tried to make jokes," Haydeez whispered. "You're supposed to be from this serious organization." She shook her head. "Lucky for us they just glossed over it."

Linx chuckled to himself. "Come on. Telling them that the Sphinx has a cold and we don't want it to spread to the pyramids is hilarious," he whispered. "You're just jealous because you didn't think of it first."

They walked quietly up the ascending passageway towards the Grand Gallery.

"Wow, you make noise no matter where you go," Haydeez said. "Your feet sound like elephants stomping around."

Linx scoffed. "I'm not that loud. You're being ridiculous," he said. He tried to place his feet down slowly to avoid any sound. "See? I'm quiet."

Haydeez chuckled. "The fact that you have to tell me you're quiet shows how loud you are."

Linx scoffed. "Don't be such a child."

Haydeez snorted. "Takes one." She paused and lifted a hand. "This is a pretty big chamber. Is this the Grand Gallery?" She looked around. "That would be the King's Chamber," she added as she pointed to the pink granite monoliths. "Let's go."

They entered the chamber slowly as if they would disturb the silence. The granite walls and roof gave the room a feeling of wonder. "If I wasn't here to find a trapped god, I would probably be taking pictures and soaking up this amazing place," Haydeez said, her voice barely above a whisper.

"You don't have to whisper anymore. We're pretty high up and far away from everyone," Linx said. "I think we're good for now."

Haydeez shook her head slowly. "No, there's something else in here. I don't know what it is but something is trying to get my attention. If I talk too loud, I won't hear it," she said. She walked slowly around the chamber in an attempt to locate the voice. She closed her eyes and touched the empty sarcophagus. "This chamber is a lie," she mumbled. "It's not real. I mean, it's real but it was never meant to be a tomb. It was meant to be a temple."

"So, he's here then," Linx said.

"No, well, yes, he's here. We can't see him yet," she answered. Her fingers slipped over the edges of the sarcophagus. "Bodies were sacrificed here." Her eyes traveled around the room. "The small shafts to the outside, they allowed souls to go straight up to the gods. I think that's what I'm seeing. There are no words, just images, but I think killing people in here is pretty clearly a sacrifice." She furrowed her brow. "Get your camera into the shafts to get those markings so we can get out of this place." She paused. A gasp escaped her lips. She put her hand over her mouth. "He's not up here. He's down below."

"Wait, what you mean? He's in the Queen's Chambers? But there are no markings in there," Linx said.

"You're right, but what about the sub-chamber under the pyramid?" she asked. "I don't know what those markings are or what they're for, so just get them in case we need them but I think he's down below. Don't ask me how I know but there's more to this place than we know." She turned to leave the chamber. "Just meet me down there when you're done. Don't take too long. I don't want to be here longer than I have to be. I have a feeling something is not right."

Linx nodded and turned toward the first shaft. "Shouldn't take but a few minutes," he said and fed a tiny camera into the entrance.

Haydeez crouched down and made her way back down the tunnel they had come up. She passed the turn for the Queen's Chamber without a second glance and continued further down. When she reached the hallway to the entrance, she stopped. Her heart beat steady as she took a deep breath. She poked her head around the corner to ensure the guard was not there. Nobody stood in the hallway, no voices could be heard from outside. She was alone.

She turned quickly and raced down the darkened pathway beneath the massive pyramid. Goosebumps danced up her arms the further she went down. It took several minutes to reach the actual chamber but when she did, her mouth dropped. She shined her flashlight around the unfinished chamber.

"What the..." she started to say. "Did you really use this for transport to the afterlife?" she asked. "This is amazing." She took a few steps into the chamber and looked around. "Where are you locked up, Ra? Where did they put you?" She took a few more steps and stopped. "Please don't tell me you're down the hole." She got down on the ground and crawled to the hole. With the flashlight tight in her hand, she leaned over the hole and looked down. "Wow, just wow," she mumbled.

She pulled her body back from the hole and stood up. With a sigh, she brushed the sand off her pants. "Ok, so where is the key? How do I let you out?" With her eyes closed, she let out a long steady breath and just listened.

The subterranean chamber was completely silent. Haydeez could hear her heartbeat, slow and calm, but nothing else. "Come on. You have to be here. I can't be wrong about this. It's the only thing that makes sense. I could see what they did upstairs. You're not there," she whispered. "Please show me where you are. I want to let you out."

The stones and sand around her settled as if the whole place was alive. "I knew you were here," she said. "I'm going to get you out. We'll figure this out and we're coming back to get you." She smiled and opened her eyes.

On the ground a circle of darkness sat quietly to mark the abyss. Haydeez furrowed her brow and cocked her head to the side. "Wait a minute. That's not really a hole." She bent down again and touched the edge. "You see what you want to see. If your mind believes it's a hole, that's what will be right in front of you," she mumbled. Her fingertips skimmed against something cool, solid. She giggled. "It's a door. There's a door under the pyramid."

"Haydeez. Are you alright?" Linx whispered around the corner. "What are you doing down there?" He asked and ran up to her.

"It's a door, Linx. This is a door. Touch it. I can feel it," she whispered. "It's been here the whole time. I have no idea how long he's been down here but this is definitely it. I can't believe we found it. I just need to figure out how to open it now." She looked up at him. "Did you get the markings?"

He reached down and took her hand. "Yup. We really should be getting out of here now, love. They might be wondering what's taking us so long and you don't want them to come looking for us." He looked over his shoulder. "Come on. We need to get out now. Something isn't right. "

Haydeez stood up with a smile. "We found it, Linx. Aren't you happy?"

Linx smiled back. "Of course. Now we have to figure out what all this says so we can let him out."

A rustle sounded and they both turned to face the pathway. "What was that?" she asked.

"No idea," he said and took a step towards the opening. He tried to peek around the corner but quickly jumped back. "Snake! It's a snake. Really huge snake!" he yelled.

"A snake? Why is there a snake in here? It can't be that big," she said. "Let me take a look." She started to walk to the opening but stumbled back when a snake began to slither around the corner. "What the hell? That thing is huge!" she yelled.

Linx turned to her. "I know! That's what I said!"

The ground began to vibrate as the snake slithered towards them. "I cannot permit you to be here. It is not wise for you to interfere," it hissed. "Your fight does not involve him. You should leave now."

"Talking snake," Linx yelled. "Why is it talking?"

"Wait. You're one of hers, aren't you? Pandora let you out," she said. "That's the only thing that makes sense. Ordinary snakes don't talk but creatures do." She looked at Linx. "Snakes from mythology? Any ideas?"

Linx looked back and forth between Haydeez and the snake and scoffed. "Without my computer I have no idea. Whatever it is, it's not good. Is that blood?" he asked.

The snake flicked its tongue. "I had a little snack," it hissed. "I did not need anyone behind me while I handled you down here." The ground vibrated again. "Now, I can deal with you in peace."

Linx threw up his arms. "It killed the bloody guards outside. Well, I guess we don't have to worry about them asking questions about why it took us so long in here. I don't think I could explain to them that we had to fight a giant snake before we came out!" he yelled.

"Calm down," Haydeez said as she stepped slowly towards him. "This is one of hers. We can kill it and then we're gone. Think. What snakes do you know of from Egyptian mythology?"

A raspy laugh escaped from the serpent and the ground vibrated once again. "You will not kill me. Only one has defeated me and he is nowhere to be found." It laughed again. "I will devour you and everything in my path." It slithered into the chamber. The creature circled around almost the entire room and still had not pulled its full body inside.

Haydeez and Linx slid along the wall, careful to avoid the creature. The body was as big around as a barrel, but it moved with ease. The creature flicked its tongue again and laughed. "I can taste your fear. You are right to fear me." It turned to face them as the tip of its tail entered the room.

"Bloody hell, that thing has to be at least fifty feet," Linx said. "I'm not going to be eaten by a snake, love. I'm not dying in this pit." He kept his eyes on the snake and watched.

The creature coiled itself loosely and flicked its tongue several times. The ground shook with each flick. It began to sway its massive head back and forth.

"Do you feel that?" Haydeez asked. "I think it's causing the vibrations." She reached over and grabbed Linx by the arm, her eyes still on the serpent. She yanked him over to her and whispered, "When I say go, run for the entrance. Ok? Just keep running. I'll be right behind you."

Linx pulled his gaze from the snake for a second and said, "What? No. I'm not just leaving you."

"Go!" Haydeez yelled and shoved him towards the pathway to the entrance. She had reached behind her to a small sheath and pulled out her iron dagger. In one swift movement, she jumped at the snake and slashed.

Linx stumbled and hit the wall. He rolled off and started to run. "For the record, I'm not ok with this!" he yelled over his shoulder. It took little time to get back to the entrance and out into the night air. He looked around and saw nobody. There were no bodies, no body parts, no sign that anyone had been out here at all. He threw back his head and groaned. "Right. Need to get to the car."

Inside the pyramid, Haydeez stabbed at the creature's back. The dagger barely broke the skin. "Damn it!" she yelled.

The snake laughed and the ground shook harder. "I warned you that you would never kill me. There is only one who can and he is gone. Your life will end with me."

Haydeez huffed as she rolled towards the snake's head. "I've been hearing that a lot lately. In case you're wondering, everyone has been wrong." She slashed at the snake's head and opened a small wound.

"I only have to be right once," the snake hissed. It whipped its tail over its head in an attempt to knock her off.

Haydeez ducked and slashed again at the open wound.

The snake flung Haydeez off its back and she slammed into the wall with a grunt.

She shook her head and said, "Not the first time that's happened. Time to go now." She jumped up and turned towards the pathway outside.

The snake rolled and the ground began to rumble. "For that I will eat you slowly so that you will feel the pain longer." The rumbles grew stronger.

Haydeez stumbled but continued to run. "Please don't fall on me. Please don't fall on me," she said as sand and granite dust rained down on her. "This is not good. I don't want to be buried alive in here." She saw the light from the moon and pushed harder. "Thank you, thank you, thank you. Linx!" she shouted. "Where are you? We need to go now!" She held the blade tight in her hand as she ran.

Lights flashed and Linx swung the passenger door open. "Let's go!"

Haydeez jumped in and slammed the door with her free hand. "Move, move, move," she shouted.

"Think you could put that away now, love?" Linx asked as he motioned to the dagger.

"Nope. It's got blood on it. Maybe Lian can figure out something to neutralize or tranquilize or something," she answered. "I don't want to wipe it off yet. We have to figure out how to kill it though. It just ate all those guards like candy and kept going. That's not normal."

Chapter 12

"This should help to keep what she has left until we can get the rest back," Keeglian said. He placed a metal bracelet around Agent Blue's wrist. The weight of it made her hand fall. Agent Red gently grabbed her arm and pulled it back under the blanket. He wrapped his arms around her and pulled her closer to his chest again. He closed his eyes and sighed.

"If you don't mind, Mr. Keeglian. I appreciate you taking me back to my home. I'd like to take a look through some of my books," Cornelius said. "I believe there may be some information to help us."

Keeglian motioned to the door. "You did leave the door open as I asked, correct?"

Cornelius nodded.

They walked to the bathroom. Keeglian drew a few symbols and knocked. "After you," he gestured. The two men walked through the door and closed it behind.

The room grew silent. Linx watched Agent Red from the corner of his eye. He pretended to look at his computer screen but instead he witnessed what had become of the man who acted like nothing could hurt him. He saw how that man crumbled at the possibility that Agent Blue would not regain consciousness. Inside, Linx felt the pain that man felt because he would do the same if something had happened to Haydeez in spite of the fact that they were just friends.

He stood up and walked over to Agent Red. "Can I get you something, mate? I know you can't really get up right now. Is there something I can get you?" he asked.

Agent Red shook his head slowly. "Just figure this out. That's all I need right now."

Linx grabbed a chair and pulled it over to the bed. He sat down and asked, "Is there anything else you can think of that might help us bring her out of this? Anything else that happened or maybe something that the creature did? It doesn't matter how small the details."

Agent Red turned to face Linx. "Look, it happened quickly. I don't remember much. She pulled something out to throw. I'm not sure what it was. Then, the alligator thing snapped at her, and pulled. At first, I didn't think it got her. But my lokon just dropped. After that, I didn't see anything else but her. I rammed into that thing to break its control. I grabbed her and I took off as fast as I could. That's all I remember," he said.

"Wait, what did you just say?" Haydeez asked. She scooted to the edge of her bed and looked at the agents. "What did you call her?"

Linx looked at the man in the bed and said, "He called her 'lokon'. It means heartbreaker. He called her his heartbreaker."

Agent Red's eyes narrowed. "You speak Russian."

Haydeez looked at Linx. "That was Russian?" She turned to the agent. "I knew you were Russian. I could hear it in your voice. Wait," she turned back to Linx. "If you know Russian, how did you not know he was Russian when we first met him?"

Linx glanced at Haydeez. "How many times are you going to say Russian, love? I didn't hear it in his voice at first. I was too busy trying to think of where they were from and why they were following us." He turned back to Agent Red. "I know it's incredibly nosy but seeing as how you're naked in my bed, I think we're about as close as we'll ever be. Why do you call her that?" he asked.

He cocked his head to the side and eyed Linx. "Why do you call that one 'love'?" he asked as he nodded towards Haydeez. "She is the only one with the power to break my heart. Without her around, I will be nothing. You don't want to see what nothing looks like." He turned to Haydeez. "You'll be hunting me."

Haydeez nodded. "Fair enough. Well, she's still there, so we should be able to bring her back. In spite of any animosity between us, I don't want to see her die. So, for now, we keep her comfortable until we can fix her. Is there something we can get? Maybe some music that she enjoys that we can play? I'm sure she can hear us right now, so talking about her is not helping," she said with a smirk. "I know I'd be annoyed if people just kept talking about me being vulnerable. She's strong and vicious. She's like me. That's probably why she bugs me so much."

"You are a thorn in her side. You can't be intimidated," he said. "She hates that." He smiled to himself and looked down at her. He brushed his fingers over her forehead and leaned down.

Haydeez slid up next to Linx and bumped him. "You never answered his question, Linx," she said with a smile.

Linx sat still for a moment, his cheeks red. "I don't know. I just do. I never really thought anything of it. Did you want me to stop?" he asked quickly.

Haydeez laughed. "Relax, punk. I'm just messing with you. It's just so easy to get a rise out of you," she said and poked him in the arm.

Linx sighed. "Brilliant. Are you done having a laugh now? I'm sure there's something else we can do to spend our time wisely." He stood up and moved his chair back to the table.

She walked over to Linx. "Don't pout. I'm just having fun." She turned back to Agent Red. "Is there something that I can call you other than Agent Red? I've seen you almost naked. Seems like we're a little past formalities."

Agent Red sighed. "If you insist, you can call me Night Raven," he answered.

"Night Raven. I can do that," Haydeez said. "I'm guessing it's because of the black wings and all that. Nice. I like it. Makes you feel more human to me for some reason. Night Raven," she said again. "So, Night Raven, can I get anything for you? Do you need to get up and go the bathroom or anything? My body is naturally warmer. I could sit with her for a few minutes. I'm sure you could use a stretch."

Night Raven raised an eyebrow. "You want to take my place?" he asked. "Are you planning on using the 'skin-to-skin' method too?"

Haydeez scoffed. "Seriously?"

"Well, you said we were beyond formalities," he said. "You've seen mine," he joked.

"And that's the last time I offer help to you," she said as she threw up her arms and plopped down on the bed.

Linx chuckled in the corner. "It's fair, love," he joked.

"I hate both of you," she said.

"I appreciate the offer. It would be nice to stand for a moment. My wings curve and conform to my body but it's still uncomfortable to sit on them for extended periods of time," Night Raven said. "So, yes, I would appreciate you taking my place for a few minutes. Thank you."

Haydeez stood up and walked over to the other bed. "I bet that hurt, didn't it? Asking for help like that," she smirked. "Not used to that are you?" she asked.

Night Raven gently moved Agent Blue over onto her side and kept the blanket around as much of her body as he could manage. He slid his leg out from the covers and slowly moved out from behind her. He held the covers up for Haydeez and stood up quickly. She jumped into his place as softly as possible and wrapped her arms around the woman.

"Really, mate? Do you just say things to make me uncomfortable?" Linx asked.

Night Raven walked past him to the bathroom door in just his dark red boxer shorts and long, black, metal wings. "Yes, yes I do," he said and closed the bathroom door.

Haydeez snickered. "I totally knew he wasn't naked. I told you, Linx. You're just so easy," she chuckled. She tried not to laugh too hard so she would not shake Agent Blue's body. "And after your little comment, you deserved it," she added and stuck out her tongue at him.

"To be fair, I'm not the one who started that," he answered. "So, if you want to take it out on someone, point your ire in another direction." He crinkled his nose and stuck his tongue out in response.

Night Raven opened the bathroom door and stepped back into the room. He flexed his shoulders and stretched. His wings scraped and shifted with every twist and reach. He looked at Haydeez, "Thank you. In spite of everything between us, you have worked hard to help her survive. I feel like I should be doing more right now. I don't know what else to do to help her. I don't like feeling helpless," he said.

"Well, Keeglian said to keep her warm and between the two of us, I think we've got that covered. Feel free to grab something to eat while I'm sitting here too. I'm not going to have you collapse because you're hungry," Haydeez answered. "By the way, what is that between your wings? Did someone give you that?" she asked as she nodded towards the starburst burn between his shoulder blades.

He reached up and touched his shoulder. "It's a reminder to me of what people are capable of, and that there's always going to be someone who wants me dead," he answered. "I still feel it sometimes."

Haydeez raised an eyebrow. "Hmm, there's a lot that I don't know about you," she said. She wiggled her arm out of her sleeve and pulled her shirt off her shoulder. She turned as far as she could manage to show him her back. "This is mine. My father says it protects me and gives me the strength I need to protect others. He said he gave it to me when I was a baby because he knew there was something special about me from the day he found me." She moved her shirt back over her shoulder and pulled the blanket tight again.

"What is it?" he asked and crossed his arms.

Haydeez sighed. "Shoshoni. He learned a few things from the tribe. He's not a shaman or anything but he knows a few tricks," she answered. "He's the one that trained me and taught me about all this stuff. Actually, he's the one that pointed me in the direction of Linx originally." She looked over at Linx. "If it hadn't been for Joseph, I probably wouldn't have contacted you, punk. Now you're stuck with me," she paused. "Forever," she added in a whisper.

"I don't believe that he minds that," Night Raven said as he pointed over to Linx.

"Shut up, mate," Linx said quickly. "I happen to enjoy my job and all the freedom and flexibility it affords me." He rested his cheek on his hand and grumbled.

Night Raven began to walk back over to the bed. "Did you not want her to know that?" he asked. He turned to Haydeez and said, "I will take my place back now. It makes me feel useful no matter how simple the task. She needs me right now." He lifted the covers gently and allowed Haydeez to quietly slide out. "Thank you," he added and moved back onto the bed. Every movement was intentional. Nothing he did was accidental. He made sure that each bump or brush only served to make Agent Blue comfortable. There was so much love and compassion it spilled over into the rest of the room.

Chapter 13

Pandora stood next to a woman bound in chains. The woman slept curled up on the floor next to a large rock. She was covered in dirty, torn clothes. Bruises darkened her skin on her arms and legs. Her body shook for a moment and a tear traced a clean path through the filth on her cheek.

The phenix egg sat on the ground next to the woman. It pulsed and hummed calmly.

Pandora inhaled deeply. She smiled and laughed. "Oh, poor Apep. Your blood was spilled. It was not enough to kill you but I still feel it. I still feel your energy slipping away. Hide away somewhere to heal yourself. She will be back and she will bring someone to kill you," she said. "Your sacrifice will be remembered."

The woman stirred and tried to pull herself up. "Please, let me go home," she begged, her voice strained. Her lips were cracked and bled. "I just want to go home. I swear to you, on my life, that I won't tell anyone about you. Nobody will know what you did to me. To be honest, I don't even believe it myself. People would think I was crazy." She coughed. "Just let me go, please. I don't want to die here."

Pandora kicked the woman in the stomach. "You complain a great deal for someone who is the reason humans are still around. Well, not to worry. We will fix that soon enough," she said. "Your other half will be here and we will end your cycle once and for all. You have lived for centuries. Your time is done. We will wipe the world clean and start anew. My brothers and sisters will once again roam free."

The woman began to cry. "I don't want to die. Please don't kill me," she pleaded. She grabbed onto the rock and dragged herself closer to it. It took all the strength in her body to just sit up straight. She started to breath heavy. The tears turned into deep sobs. Her entire body shook uncontrollably. The tremors were so violent that she almost knocked herself unconscious several times. The threat of injury did not stop the quakes in her body. It appeared that she had gone into shock and that was the only way her body could fight back.

Pandora knelt down and ran her fingers down the woman's sullied cheek. "Poor child. You still do not understand. You always die. There is always something that causes it. You have died hundreds of times, thousands of times, with your brother as you held each other's hands. If I left you alone, you would continue to die and suffer, then be reborn and go through life again as someone else. You always die, but this time, you will not be reborn. The only difference is that you do not have a new chance at life next time. Your life will end, his life will end, all of humanity will end, and the world will continue to turn as it always has. The next turn will not be yours. Your fear, your pathetic requests to allow you to live, they just do not matter. Whether I am here or not, your life has to end for humans to remain alive. The humorous part is that you have to die for them to die too. It is all about the 'execution'," she said with a chuckle. "I am not certain whether or not you will feel pain because this will be the first time I have fulfilled my destiny. However, does pain truly matter when you will be an integral part of the reformation of this world? All creatures will have you and your brother to thank for giving them the chance to exist again without humans." She smiled and patted the woman on the arm. "You are important."

The woman just stared at Pandora. Her brow furrowed and her body continued to convulse. It was so rough that she could not even form words because her jaw chattered too much.

Pandora patted her again and stood back up. "It will be over soon."

Chapter 14

"Ok, so, here's the thing. From what we've read, we have to retrieve what she stole of Agent Blue's soul before we can get rid of her," Cornelius said. "If we don't, she will stay comatose forever. She never comes back from this," he added and looked around the room.

Night Raven's muscles flexed and goosebumps rippled across his skin. "And what happens if she is killed by someone else before we have the chance to do anything?" he asked through gritted teeth, his arms still wrapped around her body.

Cornelius stood up and walked towards him. "That, my boy, is the silver lining. She can't be killed in the same way as you would with other creatures. So, we have time to perform whatever it is that we need to do in order to bring this young lady back to you. What we have to do once we've recovered your lady friend's fractured soul is send Ammit to hell where she belongs. For some reason, she was trapped in the box. Ultimately, she's not good or evil. She's just there but when Pandora brought her to this plane of existence, it distorted and twisted her. She never should've stepped a foot onto this world but now that she's here, she's a terrible force that needs to be stopped."

Keeglian stepped forward. "That's where I come in," he said. He carried a large book with a dusty leather cover. It was about the thickness of an adult male finger but the pages were as thin as tissue paper. He lifted the book and said, "Within this tome is a spell that will reverse the process that Ammit uses to pull the soul from a body and consume it. The tricky part will be getting her to stay still while we perform the spell and put the soul back into the agent's body. We will need to have the lady agent nearby to put her soul back quickly. This is where we will run into issues. We cannot have her body unconscious on the ground in the middle of a fight while the rest of our group are attempting to keep Ammit contained."

Haydeez nodded. "Sounds like a good start. Now we just need to figure out a way to keep her distracted while we get that spell working," she said. "What other spells do you have in there? Anything to stop her from moving?" she joked.

Keeglian shook his head. "I have already searched for that. We would need something more powerful than what we have right now. Unfortunately for all of us, I do not have time to create one. If I had more time, I would be able to craft one, but time is not a luxury that we possess. So, for now we will just need to have everyone focused on getting her soul back into her body. Does anybody have any suggestions for how we will do this?"

"What about making you invisible?" Linx asked Keeglian. "Can we do that? I mean, if she can't see you, she won't know you're there and you can get close enough to do the spell, right?" He turned to Night Raven. "Then, you can fly her in from somewhere. You obviously fly fast enough to get away. I'm sure you can get in there quick enough to collect her soul and get out of there."

Night Raven nodded in agreement. "I would not be able to land though. I cannot risk putting her down and placing her in range again," he said. "But flying would be the fastest way out of there. How long would I have to stay there for this to work?" he asked.

Keeglian scratched the tiny beard on his chin. "I would say maybe a minute. However, you do not have to be there until the moment I finish the spell. From that second, it will take about sixty seconds for her soul to leave Ammit and return to her body," he answered. "I have worked the spell to ensure that her soul will only reenter her own body, however, if you are not in place at the right moment, her soul may wander and I am not able to stop it. This is why we will need to time this correctly. It is incredibly important to time this to the second."

"How close do you have to be?" Haydeez asked. "I don't want you to have to be sitting on her back for this. I want you only as close as you need to be. You may be able to do magic but that doesn't mean you can protect yourself in a fight. You're the only one who can do the spell, so we can't risk losing you," she said.

"That's not a problem. I can stand on top of a nearby building or around a corner but I need everyone within earshot because we will need to coordinate this correctly," Keeglian answered. "If one thing goes wrong we could lose the agent completely." He looked around the room and everyone had their eyes on Night Raven and Agent Blue.

Night Raven sighed heavily and squeezed Agent Blue a little tighter. "We have communication devices we can use, yes? I will be where ever you need me to be with her in my arms, ready to go. You do your job and I'll do mine. I will not lose her," he answered.

● ● ●

Haydeez, Linx, and Night Raven left the hotel room. Night Raven carried Agent Blue cradled in his arms. She was wrapped tightly in a blanket. Only her face was uncovered as it rested quietly against his chest. The group made their way outside to the car. Linx held the door open for Night Raven who crouched down and slid in delicately. He maneuvered his way into the seat and ensured Agent Blue was completely inside before Linx closed the door. The back door on the other side swung open and the car bounced. The door swung shut.

Linx chuckled. "Still can't believe you did that," he mumbled.

Haydeez smiled. "We might just be able to pull this off," she said. "Let's get to it." She climbed into the driver's seat and started the engine.

They headed down the highway towards the last location of an attack. Everyone remained quiet. The only sound was the hum of the engine and an occasional heavy sigh.

"I hope it's not too tight of a fit back there for you guys," Haydeez said. "I didn't plan on transporting all of us. Otherwise, I would've gotten a larger car."

"We're fine back here," Night Raven answered. "We won't be in here long. Once we get close, I will get out and circle out of sight. Just remember what part you play in all of this," he added. He stared out the window and tried to find something to focus on outside. Everything moved so quickly that he could not keep his eyes on anything. He took a long, deep breath and closed his eyes for a moment.

Haydeez glanced in the rear view mirror and said, "We will not let her down, Night Raven. Getting rid of Ammit is important but it's not our top priority on this little outing. As long as we get Agent Blue's soul back, it's a win for us." She pulled the car off to the side of the road and parked. "Time to fly," she said.

Linx climbed out of the passenger seat and opened the back door. He watched as Night Raven slid out of the seat and stood up with ease. He carried Agent Blue as if she weighed nothing. "We'll let you know when we're in place. Good luck, mate," he said and patted him once on the shoulder.

Night Raven secured the blanket and spread his wings. The black metal had a quiet, somber sparkle to it. Even the scrape of the feathers was like a soft whisper in the night air. He nodded to Linx and kicked off the ground into the air. He circled once and headed towards a small building.

With a sigh, Linx climbed back into the car. "This will work, right? I do not want to be on his bad side. I mean, I don't want her to die or anything but I really don't want to make him angry," he said.

"It will work. I know we will make it work," Haydeez said. "I have to believe." She ran her fingers over the charms and added, "Without a little faith, nothing works."

•   •   •

"We're in position," Haydeez whispered. "Is everyone ready?" she asked.

"Ready," Night Raven said.

"I am ready as well," Keeglian answered.

Haydeez nodded at Linx and smiled. "Blind faith," she whispered.

Linx smiled back and said, "Blind faith, love."

They ran out from behind the building and charged Ammit. Haydeez pulled an arrow back and let it fly. The creature snapped at the arrow with her massive jaws and laughed.

"That is what you bring to me? A pathetic arrow? I hope you do not intend to keep your soul because tonight it is mine," she growled, her voice an echo of itself.

Haydeez sent another arrow her way as she continued to charge head on at the creature. "I've never been called smart," she answered. "Plus, I really enjoy pain," she added with a smirk. "So, yeah that's what I'm bringing you right now."

Linx fired several rounds at the creature. "I bet that feels refreshing, doesn't it?" he asked Ammit. "Might not kill you but I know it's enough to annoy you a lot." He raced towards her.

Ammit growled. "Why do you puny humans insist on fighting back? You cannot defeat an eternal creature. I have always been. I will always be. When you die, I will be your judge! I will decide where your soul spends eternity!" she yelled. "I hold your future in my grasp and now, I also hold your life." She snapped at Linx.

Linx jumped to the side and fired a few more shots. The bullets ricocheted off Ammit's scaled skin on her face and neck. "Bloody hell. I'm just a mosquito to you, aren't I?" he asked.

Haydeez shot another arrow and then leapt into the air. She kicked Ammit in the face. "Hi, how are you?" she asked casually. "I hope you didn't forget about me. I'm really needy when it comes to attention. I have to have all your focus," she joked. She swung her leg around and caught Ammit on the side of the head. Her heel connected with the flesh right next to the god's eye socket. "Oops, sorry about that. I was actually aiming for your nose. Guess I'm a little off tonight." She pulled back her fist and rammed it straight into the creature's face.

Ammit turned and snapped her jaws at Haydeez. "I will take yours first," Ammit said. She paused as she sniffed the air. "Do you even have a soul? What are you?" she asked.

"Duck!" Keeglian yelled into the ear piece.

Haydeez and Linx dropped to the ground.

• •

Keeglian pulled his pocket watch out and checked the time. "I am ready as well," he said. He moved towards the edge of the building and looked around the corner. In the distance he could see Sobek but the alligator creature had no interest in Ammit. At least for the moment, he stood and watched. He saw Haydeez and Linx shoot out from a darkened alley and head straight for Ammit. They fired and shouted and made more noise than necessary but they pulled all her attention.

Then he made his move. Keeglian walked from his corner straight towards Ammit. He needed to be close enough to her to feel her aura. So, he walked. He did not run for fear that she would hear his hoof beats, and then the invisibility spell would be worthless.

The magic that flowed from her gave off an intense heat that made it difficult for him to get closer. He was where he needed to be. He glanced at Haydeez and Linx before he began his spell. The words he spoke were from a long dead language, or at least one that was thought to be dead. Humans did not know anything about it, but he was no human. The spell rolled off his tongue like a creek as it feeds into a river.

His eyes rolled back and his head moved from side to side. Then, his eyes flew open and he reached towards Ammit. He yelled, "Duck!" and started to pull an invisible tether towards himself.

Night Raven shot down from the sky out of nowhere. He dove straight for Ammit.

As Night Raven reached the creature, Keeglian pulled Agent Blue's soul through Ammit's massive teeth.

Keeglian held on tight and pulled with all his strength. "Scoop it!" he yelled to Night Raven.

In one swift movement, Night Raven swooped down and almost scraped the ground when he pulled up. He spun and twisted right up in front of Ammit. The tether that Keeglian held onto snapped and wrapped around Agent Blue.

Ammit gagged and thrashed. She growled and tried to snap her jaws but could not get them to close as long as that soul tried to escape. "No!" she snarled. "That soul belongs to me now!" Her words were caught in her throat as the last part of the soul slipped out.

"Now!" Night Raven yelled and flew straight up into the sky.

"Get her far away!" Haydeez shouted and swung her leg out to kick Ammit in the stomach.

Keeglian took another step forward and began to chant. The winds began to pick up and swirl around Ammit.

The creature looked all around herself and yelled, "What are you doing to me?"

"Sending you back to hell," Haydeez answered. She rolled to the side and bumped into Linx. He fell to the ground. The winds whipped her hair into her face. "Time to move back!" she yelled and pushed him.

Linx nodded as he tried to get up. The wind knocked him over, and he fell backwards. He tried to catch himself, but he fell hard and knocked his head on the ground.

"Damn it!" Haydeez yelled. "I'm not carrying you. You better get up, punk!" She grabbed his arm and pulled him into a seated position. "We need to get away from this area or we'll be sucked in when he opens that thing." She squeezed his face in her hands and tried to get his eyes to focus on her. "Crawl if you have to but we need to get away from here!"

He tried to nod but his head just wobbled. "Roll me that way," he said and nodded towards the buildings. "I can roll there." He dropped onto his side and tried to roll himself like a log to the nearby alley.

Haydeez scoffed as she stood up. She grabbed him and tossed him easily over her shoulder. "I really didn't want to carry you today. I'm not going to let you forget this!" she yelled. The heat from Ammit's magic and the portal began to weigh heavy on her shoulders. She groaned. "Ok, need to be quick," she said to herself and ran towards the alley.

Keeglian stood hidden from everyone's view amidst the storm. He continued to chant.

A red light began to swirl behind Ammit. It expanded and pulsed over and over until it was the size of a car. The red light turned into flames and flickered around the swirl. A portal opened and Ammit started to slide backwards into it.

She shrieked. "I will not go back there! I have so much more work to do here! I do not belong there! I belong here where I am needed to cleanse this realm! Release me!" She scraped at the ground in a feeble attempt to pull herself out of the portal. She howled in pain and screamed, "No! I will return! I will find another way out and I will finish what I started here!" Her body jerked backwards and shot straight into the portal. It disappeared and the portal snapped shut immediately.

Chapter 15

A rock crashed against the wall of the cave. "How did this happen? Where is my power? If she is gone, I should have the power!" Pandora yelled. "I want my power!" She threw another rock. It hit the wall and cracked.

The young woman in chains said, "Does this mean you can't kill me now? Do I get to go home?" she sniffled.

Pandora backhanded the woman. "No, Pyrrha. You will still die. If I have to release every evil I have trapped in here," she said as she motioned to the disc. "I will gain enough power to destroy man. It will happen." She began to pace. "I abhor these emotions. Humans have such a loss of control when it comes to their emotions. I cannot see how they wake up every morning with all these 'feelings'. It is such a waste of time and energy." She took a deep breath and let it out slowly. "No matter. I will make this work. There are many other creatures just waiting to be released."

Pyrrha cradled her face as fresh tears began to fall. "My name isn't Pyrrha. It's Joanne and I still don't know who you are," she said.

The disc began to glow. Pandora smiled as she ran her fingers over the symbols. "Who wants to come out and play?" she asked. "Who wants to run free through this world and devour everything in their path?" She stopped and her eyes grew wide. "Yes, there you are. With your strong skin, you will be difficult to kill. When you take a life, you take everything with it. The more you devour, the more powerful you become to me. The longer your rampage lasts, the more I gain. Yes," she said slowly. "I will release you. She will have to figure out how to kill you and then I will take your essence." She turned and walked out of the cave.

•   •   •

"Be free, great Manticore!" Pandora yelled. "Kill! Decimate! Take everything! Nothing can stop you!" She spread her arms wide and laughed.

The creature stretched its wings and roared. The sound of trumpets vibrated the sand dunes. The manticore flicked its tail and began to pace. It snapped its jaws and folded down the leathery wings. The creature stood as tall as a horse with a barbed tail. It shook its head like a cat.

"You are magnificent, my friend. I am giving you the freedom and ability to feast on any flesh you can find," Pandora said. She stood still and eyed her work for a moment. "I should have released you first. You are so much more powerful than the others who have failed me. You are strong. You are cunning. You will not disappoint me."

The manticore stopped and roared again. The trumpet sound was deafening.

"Yes, my friend. Of course you will be able to take whatever you like. There are no limits for you today," Pandora promised. "You may feast until you burst."

It flicked its tail, turned away from Pandora, and bounded away.

Pandora just laughed.

Chapter 16

"Is everyone ok?" Haydeez yelled. "Can everyone hear me?" She turned to Linx. "Can you see straight?" she asked as she held his head in her hands. "Hey, can you see me, Linx?"

He swatted at her hands. "Yeah, I can see you, but are there supposed to be three of you?" he asked. "Because I'm ok with it," he added with a chuckle.

She let go of his head and groaned. "Ok, so you're fine. How about everyone else? Can anyone else hear me?" she asked again.

Keeglian turned the corner and said, "I am unharmed. Good to see you, duckie." He heaved a heavy sigh and added, "Ammit has been returned to the afterlife where she belongs. I think we finally figured out how to stop Pandora from getting too powerful. We banish whatever she lets out. If we send it back where ever it came from, we don't give her any power. She said that she gets her power when you kill the creatures, am I correct?"

Haydeez nodded. "That's what she told me. I don't think she was counting on us finding another way to do things. I hope she's mad right now. That would make me happy," she said with a smile. "Hold on. I'm really confused. If the box is supposed to be a prison for all these creatures, how were we able to put Ammit somewhere else? Was that the real Ammit? Did she pull her essence from another plane and bring her here? I heard her say that she didn't want to go back to her own plane. How is that possible?" she asked.

Linx pulled himself up. "Aw, only one Haydeez now. Too bad," he joked. "What are we talking about?"

"We'll figure everything out later," Keeglian answered. "Have you seen the agents?"

Haydeez shook her head. "Not yet. Hey, guys, can you hear me? Are you alright?" she asked again. She threw her arms up in the air and groaned. "I really hope you guys are out there!" she yelled.

· · ·

Night Raven held Agent Blue's body against his chest as he flew straight up. The air grew cold and thin and he stopped. Their bodies hovered for a moment. He looked at her skin and felt her heart beat against him. His body turned, and they started to drop back to the ground.

The black wings spread wide and caught a current of air. "Far away. We will go far away from here, lokon. She will not take all of you from me," he said. His accent grew thick as the façade dropped. Nobody was around to hide from, to pretend for, to fear.

But they did not make it far before he had to drop to the ground. Agent Blue's body began to convulse in his arms. The wings folded and they fell quickly. When they landed in the sand, he dropped down to the ground and held her body tight against his in an attempt to calm her tremors.

Her entire body shook violently for several moments. Then, it stopped abruptly. She gasped and her eyes flew open. She tried to push against him and get up. "No! Leave me alone!" she shouted.

"Lokon, it's me," he said. "It's just me." He repeated the words over and over as she thrashed around.

It took a moment for her to hear the words. She blinked several times and squinted. "What happened?" she asked. "Where am I?" She blinked again and touched his face gently. Her fingertips ran over his cheeks and lips. "Love bird, you're here," she whispered. A heavy breath escaped her lips. "I don't know what happened. It was like I was in two places at once. I could hear you but I couldn't feel my body and everything was cold. I was so cold," she said and slid closer to him. "Where did I go?"

Night Raven wrapped his arms tighter around her body and pulled her head close to his heart. "You were here the whole time. I had you here. That's all I know for sure," he said.

They remained in the sand for what seemed like hours. Night Raven held his world and refused to let go. She gripped his arms and silently cried into his chest. He did not speak. He gave her the time she needed to let the trauma out. There were no words needed between them because nothing he could say would repair the damage done tonight.

A voice shouted in his ear over and over. He ignored every word. At that moment, nobody else mattered. He knew that he would wait as long as she needed right there in the sand. When she was ready, he would know. She was back, and that was all he needed.

• • •

"Damn it! Where are they?" Haydeez yelled. "You saw him get away, right?" she asked Keeglian.

He nodded. "He went straight up," he said.

Her phone rang. "Hello?"

"I hope everything went well," Cornelius said. "I have decoded the markings for you. Surprisingly, it didn't take long. It's an inscription to keep the door closed. Ra is trapped between here and the afterlife. It's like they built a hallway between the two worlds and closed the door on either end. He's basically walking around a long antechamber for eternity." He paused. "Is everything ok?" he asked.

Haydeez sighed. "Well, we got rid of Ammit without killing her but now we can't find Night Raven and Agent Blue. I don't know where they went and I have no idea where to start," she said with a groan. "I really hope something didn't happen to them after we just got her soul back."

"He's not answering? I would say just keep trying on your way back here. The sooner we release Ra, the sooner we can go after Pandora and stop her completely," Cornelius said.

Keeglian raised a finger. "If I may interject, that would not be wise. As we are standing here right now, there is another creature in the distance that is taking out buildings and starting fires. Perhaps that one needs to be dealt with before we leave the area. It would be unwise to just allow it to continue on its rampage, correct?" he asked.

"Ok, so we'll go deal with that one too and then we'll head back to release Ra. I can't leave this thing out here right now," she said. "Regardless of what happens, that one will still be out there. They don't just go away when we stop Pandora. It's going to continue to kill if we just leave it alone. We can't let that happen."

"If we don't release Ra to stop Pandora, none of this will matter," Cornelius said. He sighed. "Just take care of it quickly so we can get this done. We don't know what else she's planning right now."

"We'll call when we're done here," Haydeez said and ended the call. "Keeglian, go back to the car and keep trying to reach Night Raven. Let me know when you hear anything at all. Linx and I will go after the other creature and get that out of the way. Then, we'll head back and get our light god. Easy, right?" she said.

Linx laughed. He held out his arm and said, "Shall we, love?"

Haydeez watched as the creature turned its head and guided a beam of light from its forehead across a building and split it in half. "What the hell?" she whispered. "You've got to be kidding me right now. This thing is an alligator with a laser coming out of its forehead. If it wasn't so scary to look at I would be laughing right now."

Linx looked at the creature. "Laughing at what?"

"It's something out of a bad spy movie," Haydeez said. "How do you not see that?"

Linx shook his head. "Nope, not seeing it. Sorry. Can we go kill it and get this over with now? I don't want to be here long enough for him to notice us and then turn that thing in our direction."

Haydeez rolled her eyes. "Ok, fine. So, if you can get his attention in one direction and I can come up from the other side, I should be able to get him in the back with this," she said and held up the stone dagger. "I don't know what else will work but this dagger is our best chance and the most likely thing to work. I don't like what it did to me but at least I'm not alone this time. So, if I pass out, just carry me back to the car and get me to the hotel." She smiled. "Sound like a plan?"

Linx furrowed his brow. "Sure. It sounds like a bad plan with holes and potential problems for you, but why not?" he answered with a huff. "Is there another way to do this?"

She shook her head. "We don't have time to figure out what else will work on this one. We've seen what it can do to 'higher beings', so I say we use it now too. This is supposedly a god, so this dagger is our best hope to kill it."

Linx frowned. "Just once more, for the record, I am absolutely not ok with this. So, let's get this over with already," he said.

Haydeez smiled. "Trust me. We've got this," she said. "Go that way and just don't get shot with that laser thing coming out of his head, please."

Linx took off at a run and circled around to the creature's right side. "Hey! What are you doing?" he yelled. "You can't destroy this city! You're killing people."

Haydeez chuckled. "Wow, I'm sure he had no idea he was doing something wrong," she said as she pressed her ear piece.

"He may not have. I figured we'll start with the obvious and go from there. Usually throws them off," Linx whispered. "Please don't take too long to make your entrance, love." He turned back towards the creature and shouted, "You need to stop that now!"

Sobek stared at Linx in disbelief. He furrowed his brow and asked, "Who are you to order me to stop?" His voice boomed like thunder. "You are a mere human, a mortal. Your kind has destroyed the gifts that my kind have given to you and now you deserve to be punished for it. You have forgotten your place and we will not allow that to go unnoticed." The disc on his head began to glow. "For questioning my motives, you will die painfully."

"Anytime now would be brilliant, love," Linx said, a slight quiver in his voice.

Sobek mumbled to himself and pulled his head back. A low hum sounded and the disc grew bright.

"Now, Haydeez! I don't want to die!" Linx shouted.

The wind began to swirl around the creature. Sand kicked up and spun all around it in a blinding haze. A high pitched whistle built into a shriek.

Sobek looked around in an attempt to find the cause of the sudden sandstorm. "Your tricks will not aid you, mortal," he shouted above the wind. "You will still die."

Rocks and debris began to collect in the sandstorm. They spun around and struck Sobek continuously. He attempted to swat them away but for every one the he deflected, two more struck him. Everything moved so quickly he could not see the attacks before they happened.

As the sand swirled around at high speeds, it scraped and shaped the rocks into pointed bullets. The rock bullets fired at speeds so fast Sobek did not see them. They struck him and passed straight through his flesh. Over and over, they struck his scales and ripped into his body.

Sobek looked down at his chest in shock. Blood dripped down on to the sand and mixed into the sandstorm. There was so much blood it created red streaks in the whirlwind.

Linx backed up quickly into the side of a building. "I hope you know what you're doing," he mumbled. He slid his body along the wall and turned. The shrill noise from the wind caused him to cover his ears as he ran. He saw Haydeez and stopped.

She stood completely still as the wind whipped up around her. The dagger was in her hand, clutched tight. It appeared that she did not even see what was around her. She stared at the vortex she had created and admired it. Her lips moved and the cyclone picked up speed.

Linx turned to see Sobek stumble. The creature gripped his chest in a feeble attempt to cease the blood flow. The thick red liquid squeezed between his fingers and dripped down to the ground. It slipped into the sand beneath his feet and disappeared. Linx watched as the creature fell to the ground on his hands and knees and grasped his throat. Sobek reached out to swat at the cyclone and fell forward. He pulled himself in the sand as the rock bullets continued to pelt him mercilessly.

There was a crash as one bullet pierced the sun disc on his head. Pieces of crystal rained down on Sobek's face. His eyed widened as he caught Linx's gaze. They just stared at each other as the moments passed.

Then, Sobek's eyes rolled back into his head as several bullets shot straight through his skull. Blood sprayed out in every direction and he dropped face first into the sand.

Linx stood wide eyed. The winds continued after the creature took its last breath. Bullets continued to pass through the lifeless body.

When the sandstorm finally died out, Linx walked over to the creature's body and saw nothing but a shredded piece of flesh. It has lost all form. Pandora had already drained the life force from it as well. There was nothing left to show the magnitude of what it had been. Even the shards of crystal had been turned into powder and mixed into the sands of the desert, lost forever.

Linx sighed. He turned to look for Haydeez and found her body on the ground in a heap. He ran over to her and knelt on the ground. When he found a pulse, he sighed again. He lifted her body with ease and turned toward the direction they had come earlier.

Chapter 17

Linx reached the car with Haydeez in his arms. Keeglian opened the door for Linx to place her on the back seat.

"Is she alright?" Keeglian asked.

Linx nodded. "She has a pulse. I think she'll be fine. She passed out after the fight," he answered. "I don't know what that dagger is doing to her, but I know it's not worth her losing her life for that thing."

Keeglian nodded "While I agree with your sentiment, you know that it is impossible to stop her when she sets herself on a path," Keeglian said. "She will fight you with her last breath. All we can do is stand by her to pick up the pieces if something does not go to plan. Like today, for example. If you had not been there, what would have happened? We do not know because you were right there. That is all that we can do."

Linx stood up and groaned. "We need to get back to Cornelius. This is getting way out of hand. We need to end this soon. Have you heard anything from Night Raven yet? Are they alright?"

Keeglian shook his head. "No, nothing yet. I know they flew away but I don't know how far. My guess is that they are out of range now, perhaps," he said.

"No, they can travel to another country and we could still speak to them," Linx said. "He's either not listening or something happened. If it didn't work, he would've come back to kill us. So, something had to have happened. Did you see which direction he went in at least? Maybe we can head that way and hope we get lucky. I don't know what else to do right now. Everything seems to be getting more and more complicated the further we get into this whole mess. What's worse is that we have no idea how many things she's let out this time. All we can do is wait for them to attack and hope that we can figure out how to stop them. We need to start acting on the offensive. We can't keep playing catchup."

"Hello, can anyone hear me?" a voice said in Linx's earpiece. "Is anyone there?"

Linx looked at Keeglian. "Night Raven? Is that you? Where are you, mate? We were just getting ready to look for you guys. What happened?"

"I'll meet you back at the hotel," Night Raven said.

Linx threw up his hands. "I guess we're just going back to the hotel then," he said. "Let's go," he added and climbed into the car.

• • •

The door opened and Linx helped Haydeez walk into the room. He had his arm wrapped around her and supported her. Her petite body looked even smaller next to his over six foot frame.

"I swear I'm fine," she said and plopped onto the bed. She sighed. "This is pretty much what happened last time. That's why it took me a long time to get back here. I had to regain consciousness and then make sure I could see straight before I got behind the wheel. Trying to be all responsible and stuff," she joked.

Linx rolled his eyes. "Right, because the fact that it's happened before makes this any better. You do know that seeing it in person makes it so much worse. You get that, right?" he asked.

Haydeez chuckled. "You worry too much. I've been through worse than this. Remember when I thought I was going to bleed out on the ground in front of Cernnunous? Yeah, that was fun," she said. "Then, that naked guy picked me up and Cernnunous healed me and stuff. I hardly have a scar from that." She excitedly pulled up her sleeve and poked a little pink line on her arm. "Look? Isn't that cool? It doesn't even hurt me!"

"How did you get away with not feeling pain? My arm still hurts sometimes," Linx said. "That's just not fair. I don't have a scar but I still feel it when I do certain things, like lifting and carrying you to the car after you pass out from using a crazy weather dagger that somehow takes control of you and then causes you to lose consciousness and have a hard time remembering what happened. You know, stuff like that," he added.

Haydeez laughed. "Ok, fine. I get it. Don't be such a baby. So, have we heard from Night Raven yet?" she asked.

There was a knock. Everyone turned and eyed the door.

"Did someone order room service?" Haydeez asked.

Linx moved toward the door and looked through the peep hole. He shook his head and opened the door.

Night Raven walked into the room, Agent Blue's hand clutched tightly in his. "It worked," he said. He pulled her close and hugged her. "Her soul was returned to her body. Were you successful as well? Did you banish her back to where she came from?" he asked.

Agent Blue looked around the room quietly. She did not speak and barely made eye contact with everyone. She just stood and listened.

Haydeez narrowed her eyes and furrowed her brow. "We sent her back home. Hopefully that means Pandora doesn't get power ups from her because she's not dead. She only sucks the life from the dead ones. Crossing fingers for a win on that one. I guess we just have to wait and see. Hey, so what's wrong with you?" she asked Agent Blue. "You're normally all angry and chatty and you try to tell me what to do and stuff. So, what's going on?"

Agent Blue looked up at Night Raven, her eyes wide. He nodded slightly and squeezed her hand. "I think I've been to hell," she said. "And I don't know how to take it."

Haydeez cocked her head to the side and said, "I see. So, that's fun. Ok, now what we're going to do is not talk about it. Do I want to know what it was like? Yup, sure do. Do you want to relive it right now? I'm going to say that's a hard no. So, if you want to talk, fine. If not, then we'll just have to live with not knowing. Obviously, it had an effect on you. Right now is too soon and that's it." She shrugged her shoulders. "Right?"

Agent Blue nodded. "Right."

"Oh, I do have a question though," Haydeez started. "If he's Night Raven, what are you?" she asked.

"What?" Agent Blue asked. She looked at Night Raven. "I thought I imagined that. So, were you also walking around in your boxers or did I actually imagine that?"

Night Raven pointed to Keeglian and said, "That one told me you needed to be kept warm or you could slip into a coma. Body heat is the best. We had to share heat." There was no embarrassment on his face. "I removed our clothing and wrapped us both in blankets to trap the warmth for you." He nodded at Haydeez. "She helped at one point when I had to use the bathroom. She took over for me."

She turned to look at Haydeez. "You took off your clothes to keep me warm?" she asked with a raised eyebrow.

Haydeez chuckled. "Was it good for you?" she asked with a wink. "Just kidding. I wasn't about to get naked for you. I wanted to save your life and all but that was a little beyond what I was willing to do, no offense."

Agent Blue shook her head. "None taken. Not exactly my style either. Too short and not enough muscle for me," she answered. After a pause she said, "But thanks, for watching out for me and all that. After everything, I'm surprised you even cared enough to help. Most people would've just left me for dead and wouldn't think anything of it. You're very strange. I don't think I've met anyone like you. If it had been me, I don't know if I would have acted the same." She sighed. "I'm sorry."

"For what? Being yourself? Trying to intimidate me? Who cares about that? It's your job," Haydeez answered. "I don't exactly make friends with most people. Even Linx finds it hard to be around me sometimes. It's not a big deal. Doesn't hurt my feelings but you should probably know that a lot of it had to do with the fact that he showed some humanity," she added and motioned towards Night Raven. "I probably would've just let it go but he showed me that you guys are actually human and not some robotic color guard." She smiled.

"You're welcome," Night Raven whispered to Agent Blue.

"So, how many have you killed while I was out?" she asked.

He shook his head. "None. I didn't get the chance to yet," he answered.

Agent Blue scoffed. "Slacker," she said with a smirk. She turned to Haydeez and said, "Checkmate. You can call me Checkmate, as in 'Looks like you have nowhere to go and I'm about to kill you. Checkmate'."

"Interesting," Haydeez said. "Is that your given name or your superhero name?" she joked.

Checkmate smiled. "It's on my birth certificate."

Haydeez laughed. "Nice. I'm named after the god of underworld because he saved my life when I was born."

"Nice," Checkmate said. "Just so you know, this doesn't mean we're besties and that we're going to stay up all night doing each other's hair and all that crap."

Haydeez nodded. "Agreed."

"But pillow fights are not out of the question, right?" Linx asked with a smirk.

Chapter 18

"We have called this emergency meeting today because it has come to our attention that the prime directive of one of our branches is now in jeopardy," the Venerated One said solemnly. "We, as the Council, have been charged with protecting the prisons of those who threaten the sovereignty of our collective faiths. Over the centuries, our predecessors have successfully kept those prisons secret, hidden from the world but right there in plain sight. Now, under our watch, there have been not one, but two of those prisoners released!" he yelled and slammed a fist on the solid oak table. "This is unacceptable!"

The men at the table all nodded in agreement but nobody wanted to take responsibility. Several said that yes, it was unacceptable. Others just nodded and furrowed their brows.

"Who would like to explain to me how this is happening to us now when this was never a problem before?" the Venerated One asked. He looked around the table and waited for a response.

One man spoke up and said, "I believe that it has happened because of Peter's dog. The hunter released one of them and probably started off a chain reaction to release the others. Who knows how many more she will let out!" he shouted.

"Don't you dare blame me for this!" Peter shouted. "We all agreed to use her and you cannot feign innocence in all of this! It was your wizard who initially failed to keep her from that island! If anyone is to blame, that failure should fall squarely on your shoulders," he sneered.

They began to argue until the Venerated One slammed his fist onto the table again. "Enough! When one of us fails, it falls on the entire Council as a collective failure. We are all to blame for this and we will all be involved in correcting this egregious mistake. Are we now in agreement, gentlemen?" he asked.

Everyone at the table nodded.

"So, where do we go from here? How do we continue to protect these prisons from breakouts? These prisoners will threaten the very fabric of our faiths if they are permitted to walk amongst people again," he said.

Peter raised his hand and awaited acknowledgement. "Thank you, Venerated One. I am not sure that I know who else has been released. Could you please share that with us? I know of the one in Ireland but that is all," he said.

The Venerated One sat down at the table. He placed his fingertips together and touched them to his lips. With his eyes on Peter he said, "The dragon, Tiamet, has broken free of her prison beneath the sands of the desert. It would appear that a series of earthquakes cracked the foundation of her prison and caused the walls to crumble completely. Once she escaped, we lost her completely. We have been unable to locate her thus far." He paused for a moment and held his stare. "Are you now thoroughly informed?" he finally asked Peter.

Peter bowed his head. "I apologize, Venerated One, for not being better informed prior to our meeting. I will not allow that to happen again," he answered.

"See that it doesn't," he answered with a sneer. He turned his gaze back to the rest of the table and said, "Now, not only do we have this crisis on our hands but it would appear that we also have an unknown issue plaguing the world. Something is happening in Egypt right now that is allowing multiple creatures to roam free and decimate the area. Cities have been burned, people are being eaten whole, and we know nothing about this. It would appear that, once again, a certain hunter seems to be at the heart of our situation." He paused and looked around the table at each individual man. "Now, I am not implying that this hunter is the cause of our problems, but I am telling you all that I will not accept having someone in my employ that is more of a liability. With that being said, can anyone offer a solution to our dilemma?" he asked.

The men all looked at each other and the whispers began.

Chapter 19

"Well, we could use our international government credentials to get in and do the spell that way," Checkmate said. "After what just happened, I'm sure they've increased security and your CDC badge won't be enough anymore. It's not good to dip into the same well twice. Plus, you'll probably need to stick around here to search for Pandora because, once we free Ra, we'll want to get this done quickly. No reason to wait around for her to let something else out or figure out a way to let Ammit back out," she said and crossed her arms.

Haydeez shook her head. "Not an option. You can't do the spell. I at least have to go with you. Besides, what are you going to do when you open the door? Have you ever released a god from a prison before? Because I have. We need to be careful with this. We need to make sure he's on board with this, otherwise we're toast. He's supposedly a good god but after being trapped by humans for however long he's been in there, there's no telling what his attitude is going to be." She stopped. "Wait, it's not going to matter. This sounds awful and all, but the guys that were there before were eaten. Nobody knows about the CDC badge. Not to mention if I come back there with both of you, it lends a lot of credibility to my story."

Night Raven nodded in agreement. "This is true. If they believe there's some kind of virus in there, they will probably leave us alone as long as we need. We just have to hope that the giant snake does not come back to interrupt us while we're down there. We can't stop the spell to fight," he said.

Haydeez pointed to Night Raven. "Exactly. But if it does come back, having me there to work the spell while you guys keep that snake thing busy would be helpful. It seemed to know that Ra was trapped down there and from what I've read, if this is actually the same snake, it probably doesn't want us to let Ra out. According to the stories, that snake, Apep, is the enemy of Ra and they would fight every day. The stories say that Ra could not allow the sun to rise until he defeated Apep. They were basically immortal enemies. So, it's best to keep him away from the doorway until I can get Ra out of there and then Ra can possibly kill him for good."

"I'll stay here to keep an eye out for possible locations for Pandora. Cornelius and I can check news stories and weather maps and stuff. With Keeglian back at home, the extra eyes are helpful," Linx said. "By the way, did you ever call Peter about the kill? Be nice to get paid and all."

"Crap, give me a minute. I need to make a call," she said and walked to the bathroom. She pulled out her phone and made the call. "Hey, it's me. Both jobs are done." She paused. "Well, the pair of serpopards were done a little bit ago but that other one, I had to use other means to stop that one. It was interesting to say the least." She paused again. "No, I don't have a body to show you but I can guarantee that it's gone and will not be back again. Yes, you can charge me if it comes back to kill people again." She rolled her eyes. "I'll be waiting impatiently for my pay to post. Hugs and kisses, Peter," she added sarcastically.

When he hung up the phone, she stuck out her tongue at the phone and sneered. "I really hate you," she said and groaned. "I really wish I didn't have to work with you, but your Council pays a lot of money," she mumbled.

Her phone made a noise to notify her of a transaction. She checked her account and the money had been deposited for both jobs. "It's been a 'pleasure' doing business with you, Peter," she mumbled. "And I definitely use that term loosely."

She walked out of the bathroom and waved the phone. "Done, and paid," she said. "I really hope that's the last time I have to deal with him on this trip. I don't know what I'll do if I get another call from him while we're still here. I really do believe that he stays up all night thinking of new ways to get under my skin and then he practices his little speeches in the mirror for maximum annoyance. I think I hate him because he gets under my skin. Ugh, he's just so smug and haughty. You know, he talks to me to like I'm his dog or something, although I don't know anyone who treats their dog as poorly as he treats me, but whatever. He's a jerk and I hate him."

Everyone in the room eyed her. Linx raised an eyebrow. "Is the tirade over, love?" he asked.

She just stood and looked at everyone for a minute, then said, "What? Like nobody here has ever just hated someone. I find that hard to believe." She turned to Checkmate. "You can't tell me you haven't hated anyone, because before we became besties I'm pretty sure you despised me," she added. "And I think, deep down, you might still hate me just a little."

"Right now, yes, I think I do," Checkmate answered. "You're a little crazy right now."

"Can give most a minute. I need to place a call," she said and walked to a corner of the room. She pulled out her phone and made the call. "Hey, it's me, tell the boss the job is done. She paused. "Well, me part of say reward was done a . . .

Checkmate, Night Raven, and Haydeez stood outside the car near the Great Pyramid of Giza. They watched as people moved all around in the early morning light. Tours were just about to start and the three of them were about to shut down one of the most lucrative ventures in the area. The locals would not be happy.

Haydeez agreed, after a lengthy protest, to allow Checkmate to take the lead. She had worked for the government for a long time and knew the right things to say. They walked up to a gentleman in a security uniform and flashed their badges.

The man looked at them and said, "That will not get you in."

"Then I suggest you get your superiors over here now because if you don't, you could be held liable for an international incident," she said with severe emphasis. She forced a smile and pocketed her badge. "Now would be preferable, or we could wait until someone else is taken. That's up to you but as soon as tourists start to go missing, I'll be sure to let the authorities know that it was you," she paused and looked at his name badge. "Haafiz, that impeded our investigation." She cocked her head to the side and waited.

He narrowed his eyes for a second and pulled his walkie talkie out. He said something in Arabic and waited. A voice crackled through the speaker and Haafiz said, "Someone will be here momentarily. I have to ask you to wait over there please." He pointed to the entrance.

Checkmate pasted a fake smile on her face and said, "That wasn't so difficult, was it? We'll just wait over there." She turned and started to walk away. Night Raven and Haydeez followed silently.

When they reached the entrance, Haydeez snorted. "I don't think he likes you either. You don't make many friends, do you?" she joked.

"Friends tend to get in the way. I'm not exactly the happy hostess or anything," Checkmate said. She faced Haafiz and crossed her arms. She just stood there and watched him.

"He'll warm up to you eventually. I'm sure of it," Haydeez said. "He looks like the super friendly type. I can see you guys hanging out, swapping recipes, having lunch at little bistros."

Night Raven cracked a smile.

Haydeez raised an eyebrow. "Careful. You keep that up and your face will stick like that," she said.

"Do you use humor to hide your fear?" Checkmate asked.

"Nah, I use humor because I'm annoying," Haydeez answered quickly.

Another man in a security uniform began to walk over to them. He extended his hand and said, "I'm Yosri. How may I help you?"

Checkmate pulled out her badge and ignored his hand. "We need to have a look around. After the incident here, we have reason to believe that these people are all in danger. Your intern over there tried to tell me that you wouldn't allow that. I figured it was best to speak with someone who knows policy and understands the importance of keeping these tourists safe and happy. I'm sure you're one of those people, right, Yosri?" she asked.

Yosri locked his hands behind his back and looked her in the eye. "What areas will you need to investigate?" he asked.

"All of it," Checkmate said. "The entire Great Pyramid. The incident occurred here, so hopefully there's some evidence that we will be able to collect, something that hasn't already been contaminated by thousands of people touching everything here. I had hoped to already be started but, well, you know," she said and nodded towards the other security guard. "Sometimes there are speed bumps in our way to protecting people. Sometimes we just need to roll over them and keep moving forward," she added.

Yosri took a deep breath and let it out slowly. "I can allow you time within but we cannot close the Pyramid off for long. Most of these people have already paid to see the inside and we cannot have a riot break out because they are being denied entry. Money speaks louder, Agent," he answered.

Checkmate nodded. "Yes it does, but bad news coverage is a death sentence. Do you even know why all those people just disappeared, Yosri?" she asked.

He shook his head. "No. Some believe it is the gods coming down to us to punish us. I am not certain why they would see the need to do that," he answered. "However, I would never claim to understand the desires of the gods. Still, I tend to doubt those speculations."

Checkmate smiled. "I wouldn't doubt. The most outlandish ideas are usually correct," she answered. "Let's get this area closed off and we'll need all your people out of the Pyramid. I don't want anyone else around. There's already been enough contamination from tourists," she said.

Yosri nodded but kept his mouth closed. He walked back over to the other security guard and whispered to him. Haafiz looked at the little group and squinted. They both walked over and Yosri said, "Haafiz will assist with getting everyone out and closing off this area. We just ask that you conclude this investigation quickly. We can delay the tourists only for so long before they begin to demand their money back."

Checkmate looked at the men and said, "It's always a pleasure when people work together."

It did not take long for Haafiz to clear out the Pyramid. He pulled out a rope and sign that said the Pyramid was closed. By the time the trio began to walk inside, people had already gathered at the rope to ask questions. Their voices carried down the long corridor and into the many chambers of the Great Pyramid.

The trio did not even make their way up to the top. There was no point. They knew where they had to go. However, to avoid suspicion, it was best for security to close off the entire Pyramid, not just the part that was already closed to the public.

Once they were passed the first tunnel, Haydeez took the lead. Her duffel bag was slung over her shoulder and she kept her eyes forward.

Nobody made a sound except for the occasional whisper of the black steel wings beneath Night Raven's coat.

They reached the subterranean chamber and the sounds from outside had finally died off. They were alone. Haydeez placed her bag on the ground and knelt down to open it. "I'll need one of you to stand at the passage way and the other with me just in case something else comes out when we open the door," she said.

Night Raven turned and walked back to the passage way. He stood next to the far wall to see both the tunnel and the chamber in case he was needed.

Checkmate watched Haydeez pull a knife and a light out of the bag.

"This is just in case the power goes out down here. Sometimes magic pulls all the power from the electricity around you. I don't want to be standing down here in pitch black. So, keep that close," Haydeez said. She pulled out an iron dagger.

"That's not the one that makes you sleep, is it?" Checkmate asked.

Haydeez shook her head. "No, this one I'll be using to cut the mystical locks that are holding him in there. Iron disrupts magic, so," she paused and motioned with the iron dagger.

"I know that," Checkmate said. "I just wanted to make sure I didn't need to carry you out of here. That'll be a little hard to explain to them out there. It's bad enough that we'll have a whole other person with us when we leave. I'm still not sure how we're going to explain that one."

"We'll have to figure that out later. I'm just taking this one baby step at a time," Haydeez said. She took a deep breath and let it out. "Ok, let's get this done." She rolled her head back and forth and popped her neck. When she stood up, she held the dagger tight in her hand. She looked down at it and loosened her grip. There was a groove in her palm from the dagger. She had pressed so hard it left a dent. "This better work. He better help us or we're all screwed," she said.

Haydeez and Checkmate walked over to the hole, or what everyone thought was just a hole. "This is it," Haydeez said. "Time to release another god." She looked at Checkmate and added, "Just get ready for anything."

Checkmate stood back and nodded.

Haydeez knelt down and began to chant the words that Cornelius had translated. He had told her to repeat them over and over along with another phrase that weakened the lock spell. She closed her eyes and lifted the dagger above the void. Her chant grew stronger and louder. Her eyes began to flutter.

Checkmate watched as the lights flickered. There was a buzz and then a pop as one of the light bulbs exploded. She kept her hand on the light and the other on a weapon. Another bulb popped as more power was syphoned off of it. Several more bulbs popped but Checkmate did not flinch.

Night Raven stood with his back pressed against the wall and watched. His eyes shifted from the passageway to the chamber and back again. His muscles tensed beneath his coat. He flicked the buttons open. The black metal pulsed in anticipation.

Screams echoed down the passage way from outside. Night Raven and Checkmate turned towards the exit.

"Go!" she yelled. "I've got this here!"

A smirk spread across his lips as Night Raven said, "Let the count continue."

Checkmate chuckled. "I'll catch up."

Night Raven dropped his jacket and raced up the passage way. It was too narrow for him to spread his wings and it made his broad shoulders slump as he moved as quickly as the limited space allowed. He growled.

The screams grew louder the closer he got to the exit. Daylight blinked like a tiny flashlight in the distance.

He pushed himself harder and finally broke free of the darkness into the morning light. His eyes adjusted quickly as he scanned the area. It did not take long to find the source. The sun glinted off two black metal wrist bracers that covered the backs of his hands and half his forearms. He clenched his fists. When he released his hands, the bracers became metal gauntlets and claws stuck out from his fingertips.

A giant serpent, at least fifty feet long, slithered behind a group of tourists. It snapped at them as they tried to outrun it. They screamed and looked for protection but the serpent seemed to be on their heels no matter where they went. There was no escape.

Night Raven turned and ran towards the serpent. His wings spread and he took off into the air. The steel cut through the air as he sped to the serpent, like a hawk as it hunts its prey. His body swooped down and he grabbed at the snake's tail. His claws slammed into the scaly flesh.

The serpent turned its head quickly and hissed. "You will pay with your life for that!" It coiled and prepared to strike.

Night Raven held tight. "Run!" he yelled at the people. "Come and get me," he taunted the snake. "You'll just be another tick mark on my kill list."

It sprung forward and snapped at him. "You speak as if you can handle a god. You have no idea who you are fighting, petty human," it hissed again. "I am Apep! I am the destroyer of the light. I fought Ra daily. You will be nothing."

Night Raven smiled. "Do I look like the light to you? And from what I heard, you may have fought him, but you never beat him. Sounds like a lot of bluster and not a lot of muscle," he said as he raked his claws through the skin and flung the tail back towards the snake. Blood dripped from his claws onto the sand and he laughed.

The ground shook as Apep recoiled. "How dare you!" he shouted. "I am a god!" He sprung forward again but Night Raven flew aside with ease.

"The angrier they get, the more mistakes they make," he mumbled. "You are a vile, filthy, legless creature who does not deserve to live," he said.

· • ·

Checkmate watched as Haydeez stabbed the void again. Light sparkled from the hole like a Christmas light. It was such a pure light that she could not take her eyes from it. Another hole opened up followed by another until the void was covered with pock marks that glittered in the darkness.

Haydeez raised the dagger one last time and stabbed hard. She yanked it back towards where she knelt and tore open a gash in the darkness. Radiance exploded from the rip and filled the room. Every inch, every crevice was bathed in the brilliance.

A hand reached out and grasped the edge of the abyss. A soft glow surrounded the flesh as if the skin itself was lit up. When a second hand reached up, Checkmate snapped herself out of her trance. She shook her head and said, "Wow, this is a first."

Haydeez stood up and stepped back. She tucked the dagger back into its sheath and waited. "Last time this happened I lost a lot of blood. Really glad this one went a little different," she whispered.

They stood and watched as the god of light pulled himself from the darkness and stood before them. From the dull grey hair on top of his head to the armored sandals on his feet, something felt off about him. His body had a halo of light that pulsed around it. A large disc sat atop his feathered head. A bird's beak poked from his face. He wore a piece of cloth that was draped over one shoulder and cinched at the waist. Perhaps it was because his body was shorter and less muscular than Cernnunous was when he was released. He seemed old and frail and incapable of any kind of act of protection at that moment.

He looked back and forth between the two women and asked, "Who do I have to thank for releasing me from that dreaded prison?"

They looked at each other and Checkmate stepped back with her hands up. "I don't take credit for other people's work." She pointed to Haydeez and added, "She busted you out, not me. I'm just here to make sure nothing else follows you out of there." She paused for a moment and added, "I really expected your voice to be more... booming or something, not so calming."

Haydeez looked down and said, "Oh, speaking of that." She moved around the god and added, "Excuse me. I have to close this back up." She knelt down on the ground and pulled the dagger back out. With a quick slice, she opened a small wound on her hand and dripped her blood over the gash in the void. She closed her eyes and whispered a few words. The tear began to heal itself as she chanted. When she was done, it once again looked like just another hole in the ground. "Much better, and less blood this time. No blood would've been preferable, but less is still good. Now the hallway is closed again," she said and stood back up. "Yeah, you can imagine so many things but they're never what you pictured. I don't know how I didn't think of it, but I never expected the god of fertility to be naked. How did I miss that?" she chuckled. "Anyway, was there anything in there with you that we need to be worried about? Was there something there to torture you or anything like that? We need to make sure there's no chance that a creature will follow you out of there."

"Nothing else was in there with me, I assure you. I was truly alone in that dark hole for centuries. I owe you a great debt, child. I always assumed that I would live out eternity in there but you have given me back my freedom. Ask for anything and you shall have it," Ra said. His voice was crisp and soft like a clear sunrise.

Haydeez raised an eyebrow. "Wow, there are so many things I could ask for I suppose," she joked. Her brow furrowed for a moment as a thought crossed her mind. "I could ask you who my parents were or why everyone keeps acting like I'm some kind of immortal. I could find out why Pandora keeps saying that the humans will die but I'll still be around." She paused for a moment and then shook her head. "But that's not why we're here. Knowing all that won't stop the world from ending," she added and shook her head. "I need your help. I thought that this would be harder than just asking," she chuckled. "I need you to stop someone from destroying the world. I don't know how much you know of other religions or legends."

He smiled. "There is more to the worldly beliefs than you know, child. They are more connected than you think. Who is it that you need to stop?" he asked.

"We are trying to keep Pandora from destroying the world," she said.

He nodded. "Yes, when she was first created, I disagreed with everything about her. No single individual should have the power to destroy humans. We depend on your worship for our power. What would we have to gain by removing you permanently? But for whatever reason, Zeus let his anger get the best of him and figured out a way for her to kill everyone. We may be gods, but, sadly, petty jealousy is still a part of us. You are all truly made in our image, faults and all," he said. "Not everyone agreed with him. Some of them came to me to ask for help. Together we fashioned a failsafe to ensure that she could be stopped. They did not want him to find out of their betrayal. So, they had me put it into myself. I had to be the one to do it. So, yes, I am capable of stopping her madness."

Haydeez sighed with relief. "So, you'll help us then?" she asked.

The ground began to vibrate and they looked at each other.

"Night Raven went after something. I have no idea what it was but we heard screaming while you were unlocking that and I sent him out after it," Checkmate said.

"That's the snake," Haydeez said. "It came back. It had to know that we would let you out." She turned to Ra. "I guess he was nervous we would let you out and you'd kill him. We have to get out there and stop him before he eats more people."

Ra sighed. It sounded like the whisper of the wind across the sands in the desert. "I will stop him and then I will deal with Pandora," he said. "There is no need for these people to suffer the whims of an angry child." He moved towards the passageway to the outside. As he moved, he did not duck his head. The sun disc turned to vapor and trailed behind his head like a sun spike or a wisp of heat. They reformed when the ceiling was high enough again.

Haydeez looked at Checkmate and followed.

When they reached outside, terrified people ran in every direction. They saw Night Raven toss the snake by its tail. He pulled back and hovered off the ground with his wings spread.

"Huh, does seeing those things in action ever get old?" Haydeez asked.

Checkmate chuckled. "He's not going to like it that he doesn't get the kill. Can I tell him now?" she asked with a smile.

Haydeez motioned over to him and said, "Be my guest."

Checkmate took off at a run and pulled something from one of her pockets. She pressed a button and held it in her hand. When she got close enough, she tossed it at the serpent's face and veered off in the other direction to where Night Raven was in the air. "We got him!" she yelled as an explosion went off behind her. She stopped and looked up in the air. "He's out and he's going to take your kill," she laughed.

Night Raven looked towards the pyramid to where Haydeez stood and saw the god next to her. His eyes narrowed. "We'll see about that," he said and flew down towards the snake's jaws. He reached down and dug his claws into the scaly flesh.

Apep snapped his jaws at Night Raven. When the teeth closed, a rumble rippled across the ground like a wave in a pond. It spread out in a circle around them until it reached the pyramid. With every snap, another vibration followed. They flowed out in currents until all the people were far enough away that they could not see who was there anymore. The tourists watched in terror as some strange man tried to kill the giant snake that had attempted to eat them.

Ra cocked his head to the side and asked, "Why has Apep returned?"

"Pandora let him out of his cage," Haydeez answered. "When we kill one of the things she lets out, she gets stronger. No matter what we do, she gets more powerful and we can't stop it because she keeps letting stuff out. That's why we need you. You have to stop her before she lets anything else out or gains enough strength to kill the world." She looked at Ra. "Sorry to throw this at you as soon as I let you out. It's kind of a crappy 'here's your freedom' gift."

Ra smiled. "You misunderstand, child. This is what I do. I protect my followers, my believers. I bring the morning to them when the darkness has taken over," he said. "Now, to deal with this abomination before he kills another." He began to walk towards Apep. He held his arms out wide and breathed in deeply. The sun disc began to glow as it pulled the light from the sun above. Everywhere else seemed to dim slightly but the sun continued to beat down on the sand where Ra walked. He made a fist and light began to collect in his hand. Slowly, a staff formed in his grasp made entirely of light. "Apep!" he shouted. "You are done here. You will no longer hunt these people. They are now under my protection." He stopped.

Apep turned to the voice he recognized. "You!" he hissed. "They released your wretched body from that prison." He laughed. "It was good to have you gone for so long, even if I was locked up as well. Knowing that you were contained made life better for me."

Night Raven sneered. "I will destroy this creature," he said.

Ra shook his head. "I believe that you will try but he cannot be killed by mortal means. You will most definitely inflict damage, but he will heal. You will tire long before he dies. And then he will consume you. I will not allow it," he said calmly. "It is my job as protector of these people, bringer of light, to destroy all things dark, such as this creature." He pointed the staff at the snake.

Night Raven growled.

"You might want to get out of there," Checkmate said. "You have no idea what he's about to do."

Night Raven grudgingly dropped the serpent and backed off. He landed near Checkmate and said, "God or not, I do not like him."

Checkmate smirked. "I know, love bird."

Ra held the staff tight as he watched Apep sway back and forth.

Apep flicked his tongue several times. "You're still weak from being trapped. I have feasted already and gained strength. You will not defeat me this time," he hissed.

Ra felt a surge of power and turned to look behind him. He saw Haydeez with her eyes closed. She clutched something around her neck and her lips moved. He turned back to the snake with a smile. "Our followers give us our strength," he said. "We do not need to take a life to gain power. We are powerful through faith." He raised the staff into the air. A beam of light shot from the end and struck Apep.

The serpent shrieked and recoiled.

Ra moved swiftly towards the creature and swung the staff in an arc. A short beam of light arced behind the staff and sliced into the snake as it made contact. Fresh blood poured out onto the sand and stained it.

Apep snapped his jaws at Ra. "You have no followers here!" he yelled. "You have no power!"

Ra smiled again. "It only takes a single spark to make an explosion," he said. Light burst from the staff and shot out towards Apep. The light wrapped around the serpent like a rope and began to tighten. "We have battled many times, Apep. We have fought until you conceded victory. Today, while we have clashed, there will be no conceding. I will not permit you to rise again. I will take your life today, giving back hope to those who feared you." The light continued to get tighter around the snake.

Apep tried to snap his jaws but he could not stretch far enough to do any damage. He tried to flick his tongue but could not reach. His eyes bulged as the realization of his demise hit him. He choked on his words as the light became so tight it started to cut into his flesh.

"Good bye, Apep. Your killing and terrorizing ends now," Ra said and yanked the staff back. As he pulled, the light that had been wrapped around Apep sliced clean through the snake and cut off his head. It plopped into the sand and blood poured out all over the ground.

"Damn it!" Night Raven yelled.

"He's going to help," Haydeez said as she held her phone.

Chapter 20

Checkmate stood in front of Yosri, probably too close for anyone's comfort. "So, what you're going to tell people is that what they saw was a publicity stunt to get more people to visit. Who doesn't want to see two 'real' gods going head to head right in front of their eyes? Are we clear?" she asked calmly. "Or would you rather have them, as well as the news crews, know the truth? We could tell them that a real fifty foot snake was here and tried to devour a crowd of tourists. That'll probably get loads of people here, right?"

"It was a publicity stunt. We're thinking of starting a show here where gods fight each other for everyone's entertainment," Yosri said. Sweat began to bead on his forehead and upper lip.

Checkmate nodded. "Well done. If people find out what actually happened here, they could be in danger," she said. "*You* could be in danger. I don't want you to be in danger, Yosri. I want you to continue your work here. Those tourists need you." She put her arm around him and smiled. "Don't worry though. We'll be sure to keep watch over you here so you don't end up in trouble. That's how much we care, Yosri."

Yosri nodded. "Of course. And I'm sure you have nothing to worry about. I don't believe that I will ever be in any trouble. I'm certain that I will be able to keep the tourists and myself completely safe," he said. He pulled out a handkerchief and wiped his forehead and face. "I swear it, Agent."

"Yosri, that's so good to hear. I love a man that can protect the people," Checkmate said. She patted him on the back. "We'll keep in touch," she added and began to walk away. She made her way over to where Haydeez was.

"Almost done here," Haydeez said. "Took me a while because the body didn't shrink down at first but I found it. This was hers and I bet she got a ton of power from it." She pointed to the all-to-familiar brand and groaned. "I just wish we could've banished this one too, cut off her supply, force her out."

Ra used his sun disc and began to burn the body to ash. "We will get to her soon enough, but we need to handle this first. Whoever this person was, they do not deserve to rot out here for everyone to see. I will burn the body the way it should be done," he said solemnly. "I have been gone too long. My followers have forgotten me. We have become nothing more than stories or legends passed down. Perhaps it is time to move on and leave this world for good. Perhaps my followers do not need us anymore and this is the way they show it to us." He sighed heavily. "I suppose that this is what happens when we are not there to guide and council the people. They turn to those who makes false promises, but not fulfill. My followers all deserved better."

"Not all of them believe in what Pandora has to say," Haydeez said. "And we don't even know if he agreed because of what she's doing. We really don't know anything. I wouldn't give up on the people just yet. I mean, look at all the people who visit this place every day just to catch a glimpse of this amazing pyramid. Think of how they would feel if they knew you had actually been here the entire time." She looked at Ra. Her eyes ached when she looked directly at him. "I think your people need you now more than they have in the past. They need you for guidance, for reassurance, for compassion. All these people have are stories, myths of what you used to be. There might be a small level of faith but most people don't believe anymore because you've been gone so long. They want to believe again but they need something to believe in." She paused for a moment and thought about her words.

"What could I offer this modern world that they can't already do for themselves? We gave them so much in the past because they had so little, but now, they have shelters that almost touch the sky. This is your time, child. What can I offer these people?" he asked.

"Look, the last god that I released gave his people back their hope. He gave them a place to belong," she answered. "There won't be as many as there used to be. Nowadays there are so many splits and beliefs that people don't know which direction to go in. Why do you think I carry so many symbols?" she asked as she pulled gently on her necklace. "Over the years, I've seen too much to believe that only one religion can be right. Just in the past few months, I've met two living gods right in front of me. You can get those followers back. You just have to reach out to them."

Checkmate stepped forward and asked, "Are you sure it's wise to encourage him to expose himself to the world? Aren't we trying to protect the secrets of our world?"

Haydeez shrugged. "Maybe it's time we just open the flood gates. Maybe people need to know what's out there. Educate them so they don't fear everything. What better way than reintroducing them to their gods? The protectors that they thought left them centuries ago."

Chapter 21

Pandora cocked her head to the side. "You've been injured, Apep. Who is taking their chances with you this time?" she asked. "Hmm, that metal human thinks he can take your life. How silly of him. I certainly hope you consume him after you are through playing with your food. Humans will never learn. I suppose it does not matter. They will all be dead soon." She picked up the egg and ran her fingers over the smooth surface. "I feel you, my son. You will reach me soon and our little family will be together." She looked down at Pyrrha who had passed out again on the dirt floor. "You do not look so good, my child. Once your brother has arrived, we will be ready to complete the ceremony. You only have a short while left to suffer," she said.

The cave was quiet except for the occasional whimper from Pyrrha. The sounds outside did not penetrate this far into the earth. The cave sat high up on a mountain with only one entrance. Snow covered most of the entrance to keep people away. Any sounds that Pyrrha made would not be heard. She had screamed and hollered over and over for help but nobody came. Her body had become so exhausted that she just collapsed into the cold dirt.

Outside the wind howled and snow blew in every direction. At that time of year, the cave was blocked to tourists. Pandora knew that they would not be disturbed.

She stood beneath a ceiling full of stalactites and admired the cave. "How perfect that we must come back here to perform this ritual. Our family has held this cave as sacred since my father was born and now his grandchildren will die their final deaths here," she said. She looked down into the pool. Stalagmites jutted up quietly from the calm waters. She heaved a sigh and smiled. "After all this hard work, perhaps I will return here to make this my home. It should stay in the family."

A shudder rippled through Pandora's entire body and a gasp escaped her lips. "Poor Apep. Your sacrifice is appreciated," she said. She took a slow, deep breath. Her body glowed with its own light. She closed her eyes. Her cheeks slimmed slightly and her body filled out more in the chest and hips. She smiled and rolled her shoulders.

When she opened her eyes, she looked down at her body and said, "Finally, a frame more fitting to a woman of power." Her clothing was slightly tight and looked as if it did not fit anymore. "Well, that is certainly unfortunate. I must remedy this soon. I will not meet my son looking like I borrowed clothing from a child. It is always important to show your best face," she said. "Pyrrha, I must leave you again. Perhaps when I return, I will bring you food, if I have time of course. I must present myself properly."

Pyrrha's eyes fluttered and she groaned. "You're..." she started and cleared her throat. "You're leaving me alone again? Please, I need to eat. You can't starve me. I need food," she begged. She was barely able to lift her head from the ground. Her only comfort was the fire that crackled and popped nearby. It lit enough of the cave for her to see but not enough for her to find her way from that spot, not that it mattered because her body was too weak to move. "Please," she cried.

"Oh Pyrrha. Your health will not matter soon. Why do you continue to concern yourself with food?" Pandora answered.

"I've been here for days. I don't even know where I am," Pyrrha answered, her voice barely above a whisper. "Just let me eat."

Pandora huffed. "When I return, if I have located food, you may eat," she answered, irritation apparent in her voice. "And now I must leave." She turned and made her way to the entrance of the cave. She left the soft cries of her daughter behind.

Chapter 22

"I appreciate the effort with Apep, I will need more if I am to aid you with Pandora," Ra said. "She has no doubt gained a great deal of power, which will require me to gain power as well. I know that this means it will take longer for me to aid you and for that I apologize. You have saved me and I should repay your bravery but I am not able to do so at this time."

Haydeez sighed. "Ok, so what do we need to do to help you so you can help us?" she asked. "Right now, you're the only chance we have to stop the world from ending. I'm not going to give up just because it might take a little longer to get it done. We just have to make sure we don't waste time. So, whatever it is, we need to speed up the process. Is that possible?"

"I need worshipers. I gain power from prayers, from sacrifices, from worship," Ra said. "If you can get me that, I will be able to stop her."

Haydeez turned to Checkmate. "Feel like heading back to the Pyramid?" she asked with a smile.

Checkmate furrowed her brow. "What did you have in mind?" she asked.

"Well, I was thinking we could get everyone up into the King's Chamber and start a little prayer session," she answered. "We could tell people that Ra will hear them best from that point in the Great Pyramid because it's closest to the sky. Make something up as long as it gets them to talk. You saw how many people were there today. Even if they don't completely believe, we make it part of the 'attack' that happened. We'll tell them it's a way for them to thank the god for saving them from the 'snake'."

Night Raven stepped forward. "That could actually work," he said. "If we could get back down there and convince everyone that they were part of the show too, we could get them to act the part and thank the god that saved them. If we get someone with a camera to pretend like they're recording it for the show, we would have to act the part."

Linx looked at Night Raven and said, "You would have to go back there and be one of the heroes, mate. You started the fight. You distracted the bad guy so all the innocents could get away. Think you can go play the friendly hero?" He smirked.

Checkmate snorted. "I would love to see that," she said and put an arm around him. "Love to see it," she whispered with a smile. "So, let's get going. I'm ready to see this in action."

Haydeez chuckled. "I can't believe we agree on something. I can't wait to see this."

• • •

Yosri stepped aside and allowed Checkmate and Night Raven to step forward. The people began to clap.

"Sometimes it is hard to find your faith. When you see bad things happen all around you, it is difficult to see all the good that is still there," Checkmate began. "But today someone stepped up to fight for you. This man here," she paused and motioned to Night Raven. "This man played the part that you needed. He kept that monster busy to allow you to run."

The crowd applauded and cheered.

"And then," she shouted as she turned and motioned for Ra to step forward. "This man here fought the monster for you! He fought to protect you! That thing wanted to kill you all but he stopped it! He is your hero today!"

The people jumped up and down and shouted. Cries of 'thank you' and 'our hero' erupted from all over the crowd. More people began to gather and watch. Soon there were hundreds of voices that praised and celebrated the man before them who they all believed was just an actor.

Haydeez quietly walked up next to Ra and whispered. "How does that feel?" She looked up at him.

Ra sighed. "It has been too long for me. I have been without this for thousands of years. I feel reborn, renewed," he said as he took a deep breath. "I feel powerful again."

"Then, it's working," Haydeez whispered. She looked at his arms and saw the dim glow gain intensity. It was like a switch had been flipped and all the praise just flowed right into him like a river. She just stood and watched him as his body appeared to grow. "We might want to end this and step back. If you grow too much people will start to question what's actually going on."

Checkmate turned to Yosri and said, "Time for us to go." She grabbed Night Raven by the arm and pulled him back. When she turned around, she caught herself. "Wow, I didn't think it would work this well," she mumbled. "Yeah, we need to leave now." She pushed Night Raven in front of her and started to leave.

Haydeez tried to grab Ra but the heat that pulsed on him was too much for her to touch. "Ra, we've got to go. You're getting too hot to touch. We need to leave before you start to burn up the people around here," she said.

Ra looked down at Haydeez and then looked at his hands. "I have not experienced this sensation in a long while. I had forgotten what this felt like," he said calmly.

"Yeah, that's great and all but we need to leave before you fry someone," Haydeez said. "I think your body is not used to it and it just heated up too quickly. We need to go." She turned to Yosri and added, "Get rid of those people now! Make them stop, go away, something. They need to leave." She waved him off.

Yosri turned to the people and said, "Thank you everyone for your participation. You were fantastic. I would like to offer you a refreshment for taking part in our trial run. Let us go this way," he said and pointed behind the people. "We will get everyone under a tent and cooled off. It is a hot one today," he lied.

The people smiled and happily turned around to head towards a tent. Yosri held his arms wide as he herded the people in the other direction. He looked back a couple times to see what had happened. The group surrounded the man who had killed the snake and tried to guide him away from the people. That was the last he saw of them.

• • •

"Nobody touch him," Haydeez hissed. "He's burning up. We need to get him out of here and away from all of this. We shouldn't have gotten so many people. I think it overloaded him." She walked by Ra but kept about a foot between them. "Wow, this is really hot. I didn't realize that you burned like this too. I thought it was just light," she said.

Ra smiled. "It is just my body's way of dealing with the worship so quickly after having nothing. The power is burning off. There is no need to worry," he said.

When he first came out of the void, he stood less than a foot taller than Haydeez. He was thin and looked weak. As he walked in the middle of the small group, he towered above Night Raven and Haydeez looked like a child next to him. His shoulders were broad, his chest puffed out and stretched the cloth that covered his body. His skin had a crisp golden hue to it that shone like polished gold. The dull greyish hair that hung limp down his back was now a brilliant blonde with streaks of red beneath like the flares that shoot off the sun. He appeared to be everything a god should be with his head held high and his confident stride.

"Well, you definitely look the part now," Haydeez said. "You were so much smaller at first, kind of like you were just human but now, you look like everything that they say a god should be. You even have the animal face thing going on. I'm glad people believed that was just makeup. I still don't get why it took a while for you to become this but the other god came out looking like he stepped off a *Men's Health* cover."

"Maybe it's because we basically brought a horde of followers to the first one," Linx said. "Maybe he just got blasted with a wave of their prayers as soon as the tree split."

"I did not have my followers inside. I wasted away to nothing. So, naturally, when the doors opened, I was weak," he answered. "Without your prayer, I may not have beaten Apep, child. You gave me strength and showed me that there is still faith in this world."

"I believe in what I can see and I can see you standing in front of me. My eyes haven't failed me yet, so I'm pretty sure I can trust that you're there," she answered. "I've seen a lot over the years and I've come to believe in more than I ever thought I would."

Ra smiled again. "Your faith, whether in your own eyes or in my abilities, has aided me in renewing my strength. Thank you, child."

With a shrug, Haydeez said, "We're fighting for the same thing. I have to have faith that we'll win, otherwise I lose hope. And I don't like to lose." She smiled. "Now we need to find out where Pandora is heading so you can stop her."

Ra nodded. "We will find her, little brave one. For now, we must return to your friends," he said.

"I have no idea how we're going to get you back. You're burning up out here, literally," Haydeez said. "We can't put you in the car. You'll start a fire and kill all of us." She turned to Night Raven. "You probably can't touch him either can you?"

He shook his head. "I would burn up. I think he has to release some of that power to stop the heat he's creating. Any idea how to do that?"

Ra nodded. "Not to worry. I have everything under control." He closed his eyes and formed the staff from earlier. He raised it above his head and started to spin it around in a circle. "Please duck your heads," he said.

Everyone looked at each other and crouched down on the ground.

As Ra swirled the staff around, a ball of light formed at the tip like a bubble. He continued to move it around until it was larger than his head. Then, he slammed the end of the staff on the ground. The bubble shot straight up into the sky and exploded in a glittery blast.

His body shrunk back down to the height it was before and the staff disappeared back into his hand. His skin still glowed and his muscles still bulged, but now he appeared to look like almost any other person, if that person had a bird mask on and a sun disk strapped to their head.

Haydeez stood up and said, "Well, that was easy, I suppose. Now we can get you into the car and you won't burn us all alive."

• • •

"Well, that's different," Linx said as Ra walked into the room. His eyes narrowed and he asked, "So, what happened?"

Haydeez smiled and said, "It worked. We actually got him more power. It was really weird."

Linx nodded his head slowly. "As much as I would like to hear more about this, I need to get back to figuring out where you need to go now that he's all fancy again," he said and turned back to the laptop. "Cornelius has been pulling what he can from the books he was able to bring with him but we're not finding much. All we know is that she will have to go back to Greece. From there, we have no idea unfortunately." He started to type again. "With just the islands alone, it could take our entire lifetime to find her. We haven't really even narrowed it down at all either." He sighed.

Cornelius nodded in agreement. "It has been a truly fruitless venture thus far. There appears to be too much ground to cover. I wish that we had better news for you but it has been incredibly trying on our end," he said. "At least we have made steps in the right direction." He motioned to Ra. "I'm glad to see that you've gained power. That will certainly assist us when we find Pandora." He cocked his head to the side. "Speaking of Pandora, what exactly is it that you will be doing to her? If she is supposed to be this eternal being, she can't be killed. So, how do you intend to stop her when the time comes?" he asked.

"It is difficult to explain to a human," Ra started. "When I was offered this responsibility, there were far fewer humans on this earth that needed to be protected. There was less of a concern of any people getting hurt. With that being said, there may be casualties from the blow but the rest of the world will remain as it is now. Humans will never know that they came so close to extermination."

Haydeez cocked her head to the side. "I'm sorry, what? What kind of casualties will there be? I thought we were doing this to prevent deaths, not cause more of them. I think she's killed enough. If more people are going to die, we need to find another way. There's no other option. I will not be the cause of innocent people losing their lives." Her phone rang. "Ugh, what now? Hello," she said and began to walk into the bathroom.

"I have a bad feeling about that call," Linx said into her ear. He looked up and watched the door close. "She never gets the 'hey, just wanted to say hi' calls. It's always the 'hey, the world is in danger and we need you to fix it' calls. I wonder which council it is this time. My money is on Peter. He's always a little jumpy and nervous. I think he's afraid that someone will find out about him and his little friends if one of these creatures is allowed to roam free. Honestly, I just want to find out where they are. I don't like them and I really don't like how they treat her." He looked back down at the screen.

Cornelius smiled and shook his head. "Are we looking for a bit of revenge, son?" he joked.

Linx scoffed. "I just don't like rude people and that's all he is."

Checkmate and Night Raven chuckled. Checkmate sighed. "Which guy was it that you went after for me? I can never remember."

Night Raven smiled. "It was Turkey. We had just finished a mission and he thought you were a waitress. I believe he got more than just a little 'hands-on'," he said. He looked into her eyes and added, "And that is when I took his hands *off*." He took her hand in his and brought it up to his lips. With a soft kiss, he said, "You never disrespect a lady."

"Well, that was a lovely and disturbing story," Linx said. "No idea why you had to tell it though. Cornelius, did we eliminate this area right here already?" he asked.

Cornelius walked over and looked at the screen. "Which one? No, we have not eliminated that one yet. I think we excluded most of the north but none of the islands yet," he said. "There are many places that we could possibly consider and not enough time to check them all. Perhaps we could come up with a better way to reject areas," he added and pointed to the screen. "Also, that was pretty slick the way you changed the subject," he whispered.

"Thank you, mate," Linx said, his eyes focused on the screen.

•

"Hello," Haydeez said. She sighed and closed her eyes. "What now?" she asked.

"If you continue with that attitude, I might start to think that you don't like me, Haydeez," Peter said through the phone.

She rubbed her face with one hand while she held the phone in the other. She leaned against the counter. "Well, Peter, I don't like you. Now that we've gotten that out of the way, why are you calling me again for the third time in that many days? I don't like to talk to you this much. It puts me in a bad mood," she said and heaved another sigh.

Peter scoffed. "I am absolutely heart broken. Perhaps money will change your feelings about me?" he asked. "I have another job for you."

Haydeez groaned. "Did you ever think that I might have stuff I need to do over here? You are not my whole life. In fact, I was in the middle of a life or death conversation when you called," she said.

"Well, being that I only call you to chat, I can see how you would want to get back to what you were doing," Peter said sarcastically. "Would you like me to let you go?"

She rolled her head back and forth and asked, "What is it this time?"

"Oh, it's nothing really. We just have a confirmed sighting of a manticore, once again in your area. Of course this leads us to believe that there's more going on than you're telling me," he answered. "So, at this point, we really feel that you should probably keep us in your little loop because it appears that you know what's happening right now."

She slid to the floor and dropped her head. "A manticore? Are you freaking kidding me? Come on, Peter," she said. "And what makes you think that I know everything that's going on? I already told you, I don't provide you with the information. You're supposed to do that and I'm supposed to just hunt and kill. I thought we had that all worked out. Have our roles changed Peter?"

"Aren't we a bit snippy today," Peter snapped. "It's almost as if you don't want to work with me anymore. I can arrange that. I could 'lose' your number and find someone else to handle my dirty work if that's what you'd prefer. You're good but you're replaceable."

"Give me a break, Peter. You're the one that calls me. You're the one that wants me. There's a reason you keep calling me back. I get the job done fast. You call me and it's done. That's how this works. You want to 'lose my number', go ahead but don't you dare threaten me," she growled. "I've had to deal with more of you in the last few days than I normally do in a month. I've been handling your problems because you can't be bothered to get your hands dirty. If you want this job done, send me information. If not, go find someone else. But just know that I will not sit here and be threatened by someone who can't even stand in front of me and look me in the eye when he speaks. So, what's it going to be, Peter? Do you want this thing killed or not?"

Peter sighed. "Not. I want it trapped. I want you to bring it to me after you catch it. Can you do that?" he asked.

"Not a chance. I will not bring you a manticore. And just so you know, not only will I not bring it to you, but if you find someone else to do this, I will hunt this thing down and kill it so they can't bring it to you either," she answered a little louder than she intended. "A trow is one thing, some imps, whatever. But I will not bring you a full-size manticore. For one, I have no way of containing it. And second, I'm not bringing you a killing machine like that. That's just insane. I don't know what you people are doing with these creatures but let me be clear: I will not bring you anything like that and I will not allow you to have anything like that as long as I can stop it."

They sat in silence for a moment as each tried to wait out the other. Haydeez looked at the phone to see if it had disconnected. "Are you still there?" she asked.

"Just kill it and be done with it. We'll be in touch," he said and hung up.

Haydeez growled and clenched her fist. She went to throw her phone but stopped herself. She set it on the floor next to her and pulled her knees up to her chest. With her head rested on her knees, she sighed. The silence surrounded her and held her tight as the minutes passed.

A soft knock pulled her from her frustrations. "Is everything ok, love?" Linx asked through the door. "Do you need anything?"

"I need to not be working with him anymore," she mumbled. "I really should just change my number. Come on in. The door's not locked." She waited for the door to open. When she could see his face, she added, "Guess what?"

He sighed. "Please tell me you're joking. Another one? You can't be serious," he said. "What the hell is it this time?"

She rested her cheek on her knee and looked him in the eyes. "Manticore. Want to hear the best part?" she asked.

"Give it to me," he answered.

"Actually, yeah, that's what he wants. He wants me to trap it and give it to him," she said with a chuckle. "He wants me to just give him a freaking manticore. Seriously. I'm not joking about this."

Linx furrowed his brow. "Is he mad? There's no way you're going to just hand over a manticore to him. What did he say when you told him 'no'?"

"Told me he could find someone else to get it."

"Wow. I can't even imagine why he would need one."

"Well, he's not going to get it because I told him that, if he did get someone else, I would hunt it down and kill it myself before that other person could get it because I'm not about to let him and his little council of creepers get their hands on a creature like that."

Linx laughed. "I wish I could've seen his face when you told him that."

"Me too," she sighed. "But now we have to find it and kill it anyway. I don't really care about getting paid. I mean, I do but, if it keeps him from getting it, I'd hunt it for a bottle of RC and a bowl of ice cream."

Linx put his arm around her and said, "Pretty sure I could have room service bring that up in the next ten minutes. Are you sure you don't want something stronger than RC?" he joked.

• • •

Night Raven and Checkmate had returned to their room to rest. Cornelius sat at the table and flipped through one of his books for the twentieth time. He scratched his head and read the same passage he had already finished just moments before that. "I can't find a thing in these, no matter how many times I go over them. Ms. Blackhawk, dear, you were the one who figured out that she is going to kill her own children. Was there anything that eluded to where those children were born? I'm sure you would have mentioned it long before now if there was, but I figured that I would ask."

She shook her head. "No, I even tried to go back through everything I had to see if maybe I missed something." She took a spoonful of ice cream and shrugged. "I really have no clue where we're going with this one. There are no stories or anything that reference her children's births or their lives. It's really weird. Usually when we're talking about 'famous families', there's a lot more information. People tend to record this stuff. So, why can't we find anything?"

Linx stuck his spoon in his ice cream and said, "What if they had to be raised in secret? So, Zeus was daddy, right? And Zeus's daddy tried to eat him when he was born. What if he wanted to destroy the evidence of what he did? He created the first humans born on this earth, right? Wait," he paused and scooted to the edge of his bed. "So, Pandora was created to destroy man but how could she be created to do that if man hadn't been created yet?"

"Pandora was created to be his companion," Ra said. He stood with his back to the room as he looked out the window. The sunlight glistened on everything outside. He breathed in deep as he took in the beauty of the sky once again. "She was not created to destroy man. Her entire purpose was to please Zeus, nothing more. Zeus asked Hephaestus for the perfect woman. That is why each of the gods gave her a gift. She was beautiful, clever, graceful, but unfortunately, Hephaestus was the creator of all weapons. Within Pandora was also deceit and betrayal. He sculpted her to look the same as any other female, however, she had the heart of a Titan and she was forged through the fires of the phenix bird to ensure she would always be there for his pleasure."

"What the heck? The heart of a Titan? Like Kronos?" Haydeez blurted. "How do you know all this stuff?"

Ra turned from the window and smiled. "Yes, child. I was there. We may not be from the same region but, as gods, we were the only ones around for so long. As I stated before, they came to me to have me hold the key to stopping her, should the need arise in the future, and I accepted the responsibility."

"I'm so confused," she said. "So, the stories are all wrong then."

"Not entirely. She believes that he created her with the help of the gods. That is why she believes him to be her father. When she was forged, Hephaestus only worked in metals and stone. To bring her into existence, he needed the power of a Titan. He used what was left of Kronos's heart to give her life. That is how she was able to create an entirely new race. Their union caused the conception of humans when she gave birth to those two children." He clasped his hands gently behind his back. "Zeus did not know of them until they had grown into adults and began to reproduce themselves. She had hidden them from him and when he found out, he was furious. He wanted them destroyed and ordered Hephaestus once again to create something. This time it was the dial that you know as the jar of all things evil. That dial she holds is a doorway, to hell, to purgatory, to the afterlife. It pulls the life force of everything evil and brings it to this plane where it can wreak havoc on those poor souls born of Zeus's indiscretions," he said. "He wanted the mother of his own children to be the one to destroy them. He felt it was not only a fitting punishment for the children, but it was also meant to punish Pandora. She has no idea what will happen to her when those children finally perish. She is essentially sealing her own fate."

Haydeez and Linx looked at each other and then back at Ra. "A portal to hell? Seriously? Bloody hell. This just keeps getting better and better," Linx said.

"Does that mean she'll die if she kills her kids? Is that what happens?" Haydeez asked.

"In a manner of speaking," Ra answered. "She will be punished for eternity for turning her back on Zeus."

"So, how are you supposed to stop her then?" Haydeez asked.

"Within that dial are the secrets to a prison in which Pandora cannot escape," Ra answered. "I will be able to trap her and keep her there for all of perpetuity. Without her dial, she will never escape. Only I have the spell to seal the door."

Haydeez turned to Cornelius. She raised an eyebrow. "How did you know he could help us? Keeglian got the information from you, right? So, how did you know it was him? Who told you he could help us?" she asked.

Cornelius looked up from another book. "I had read something that referenced a secret treaty between the gods. Since Ra is the light and Pandora is the darkness, it stands to reason that he would be able to defeat her, right?"

Her brow furrowed. "Not good enough. What are you not telling us? I've never read anything in any books about the gods banding together for anything. I've never read about pantheons crossing over except the fact that Greeks and Romans use the same gods with different names. What books do you have that nobody else on earth has ever seen before? Something is not adding up here." She stood up. "I want to know what's going on now."

Cornelius sighed and closed the book. He placed his hands on the cover and looked at Haydeez. "Everything I own has been in my family for thousands of years. Since before writing began, we have kept documentation of everything. That is the only way I can explain this to you. That is how I had that dagger and all the other pieces in my collection. They have been protected for a long time. Unfortunately, I do not have personal knowledge of some things, like Pandora for example. I am not able to locate anything in my books about where she gave birth. Perhaps, it was kept a secret from the world until the children were old enough to protect themselves. I wish I had more information for you but I do not. This is why I wanted to meet you. People spoke about how different you were and then you showed up on my guest list. I thought that perhaps I would finally have someone in my home that could help me verify the validity of everything I own. There are so many items and I'm not always able to get out. I'm not exactly a young man. There are a lot of restrictions."

"Wait," Haydeez interrupted. "What are you talking about? Restrictions on what? What people? How am I different?" she asked.

"Look, there will be plenty of time to discuss this in the future. Right now we need to figure out where Pandora is headed and make sure we are there to stop her," Cornelius answered.

Haydeez waved her hands at him. "No, I don't think so. This is just too weird for me. I don't understand any of this. I appreciate the help and all but, if there's someone out there who knows about me, I need to know who that is. If we fail and they die, I'll never know. Saving the world is important and all, but maybe it's time for me to be a little selfish." She walked over to the bathroom door and drew the symbols with her fingertip. "When you're willing to tell me what's going on, call me. Until that time, I can't trust you here." She opened the door to his home and motioned him through it.

Cornelius stood up and collected his books. "I understand, dear. I will continue to search on my end because I do not want to let you down. I had planned to share with you once this whole mess was completed. I just did not want your attention divided." He walked to the door. "I do not wish to anger you more than I already have." He took her hand and kissed it. "We will talk soon, Ms. Blackhawk," he said and walked through the door into his home.

She silently closed the door behind him. "I need a walk," she said and left the room without another word.

Ra turned to Linx. "She will be well again," he said calmly.

Linx nodded. "She's just getting overwhelmed right now. It's hard for her to sit here and try to save the world when there's so much personal stuff happening as well. She doesn't do well with 'personal'. And normally she just goes out for a ride and comes back feeling better but she can't do that here. Her horse is at home."

Ra nodded. "I see. Perhaps I could aid her by speaking to her as someone who has not been a part of any of this. I could offer her some healing words. I spent many years aiding my followers with their life choices."

"I would just let her go."

Chapter 23

The shipyards of Kolding were quiet as a middle-aged man made his way from the docks. His jacket was zipped all the way up as the snow dotted his hair. He kept his eyes forward, not even a glance to the sides. It was as if something pulled his body towards the south. He was hungry but could not stop. That same force would not allow it.

The man was no stranger to sacrifice. He would go days without a meal to ensure others were cared for and well fed. Over the years, he had taken men, women, and children into his own home when they had no other place to go. His parish adored him.

As he left the docks behind, Father Armo felt guilty about what he had left back home. Those people depended on him and he was not sure if he would ever see them again. All he knew was that someone needed him more than anyone had ever needed his help. So, he walked.

If he had known that Pandora plotted to kill him and the sister he did not even know he had, he would have fought the desire and stayed in his parish.

•   •   •

Down in a cave in the middle of a large island in the Mediterranean Sea, Pandora paced. "Where is he?" she shouted. "It should not take this long for him to arrive here." She turned to Pyrrha and yelled, "You were here almost immediately but he is taking more time than necessary! I need him here now!" Her voice boomed and she stomped her foot. She clenched her fists over and over as she continued to walk back and forth in front of the fire.

"I hope that he never comes," Pyrrha mumbled. She slowly inched her way closer to the fire when Pandora's back was turned. "I hope he fights it and never comes here."

Pandora spun around and eyed Pyrrha. Then she smiled. "It truly is sweet that you still believe that you will leave here alive, my child. Your brother will come because the desire compels him. The egg calls to him the way it called to you." She chuckled. "And here you are." She walked slowly towards Pyrrha. "You are part of a larger plan. You always have been. Your life has never truly been your own because you are always meant to die, hand in hand, with your brother. It does not matter if you come to terms with your demise. It will happen whether you want it to or not." She crouched down close to Pyrrha. "But this time, you will die at my hand."

"He will fight it and you will lose," Pyrrha mumbled.

Pandora smacked Pyrrha across the face with the back of her hand. The crack echoed throughout the cave. "Do not talk back to your mother, child."

Chapter 24

"Are you sure you want to do this one alone, love? I don't mind coming along," Linx said. He watched Haydeez put some items into her bag.

She shook her head. "No, I need you here trying to find out where we're going. Keep looking at the weather, or weird stuff that pops up, or whatever. That's our top priority right now," she said. "Sure, I need to kill the manticore, but ultimately we need to get Pandora. And right now, you're the only one that I can trust to find her. But don't get a big head about it," she added with a smirk.

"The fate of the world rests on my amazing shoulders. How would that give me a big head?" he joked. "I'm awesome and you need me."

She laughed. "Alright, soak it up while you can. I guess I can throw you a compliment once in a while."

"Are you feeling alright? Should I get you to see a doctor?" he chuckled.

"Oh, you're just so funny. You make my sides hurt from all the laughing," she said. "Ok, so, as far as this thing goes, we're sure a piece of ivory will work? That just seems too simple."

Linx shrugged. "Don't complain when you get an easy one, love. They don't come along too often. Just take it and go with it. Besides, all the stories talked about elephants being the only animal in the jungle that a manticore could not defeat. Ivory is pure and clean. No other animals in the jungle have ivory. So, unless you plan on bringing a live elephant to your fight, this is your best bet," he answered. He unwrapped a large curved piece of ivory from sections of thick paper.

Haydeez ran her fingers over the tusk. "Wow, I've never touched an elephant tusk before. I always thought it would be attached to the animal if I did. Do I even want to know how you got this?" she asked.

"If you think I went and killed an elephant myself and removed the tusk, the answer is 'no'. I would never even think to do something like that. Do you want to know where I got it, or how I got it so quickly? Probably not," he answered. "These kinds of things are not exactly harvested the easy way. I'm sure that, when the guy got this, he didn't walk up to the elephant and ask politely for it." He looked down at the ivory tusk and sighed. "I'm sorry but there really isn't another way right now." He paused. "Like I said, I can do this one for you or at least come with you."

Haydeez cleared her throat and shook her head. "Nope, I can do this alone. I just have to stop thinking about where this came from and focus on where it's going to end up. I can't let anything else distract me. Plus, I need to do this before Peter finds someone else to go after it, and they try to trap it instead of killing it. I can't let him do that. It's bad enough that I gave him that little hoko before, or the trow. I can't even imagine what he would do with it if he got it alive." She took the ivory and placed it gently into her bag. "Once this is done, I'm taking a vacation. I don't care if I stay home and live in my pajamas for a week or two. I just need to be away from all this for a little bit." She heaved a heavy sigh. "Everyone needs a break from work, right?"

Linx nodded. "I know Bebo will be happy to have you around more, even for a little while. I think a break is probably a great idea. You'll keep me updated when you find it, right?"

"Always do," she answered. "See you when I get back."

"Be safe, love."

•   •   •

"Ok, so, there's no actual evidence left behind when one of these things attacks, right? Everyone usually just attributes a missing person to a manticore. So, how do they actually know that this is what was here? There's no destruction, no bodies. It's just a bunch of missing person reports," Haydeez said. "How do we even know if the creature did this or these people just disappeared on their own?"

"That's the only information I have for you," Linx answered. "According to the stories, people used to disappear in forests and nothing was left behind to indicate an attack or a struggle. They always blamed it on a manticore. It's like they just wanted a reason to avoid going to look for the lost people or they were too scared to go out and look. I don't understand it, but didn't Peter tell you where to start?"

"Yes, but I can't track something that doesn't leave a trail," she answered. "Where am I supposed to go? What am I supposed to look for? Unless this thing is sitting next to me, I have no idea where I'm going."

Linx clicked away on the laptop as Ra stood in front of the window again. The curtains had been pulled open and he just stood there and stared outside, his hands clasped casually behind his back. He closed his eyes and soaked up the sunlight. He smiled to himself. "I had almost forgotten what the sun felt like," he said quietly to himself. "It feels like a warm embrace that can wrap around your entire body all at once." He sighed heavily.

Linx looked up and raised an eyebrow. He shook his head and said, "How about we look at where it's been and maybe we'll figure out where it's going. It could work. I mean, that's how they track serial killers, right? Why wouldn't it work for us?"

"That's the problem. I don't know where it's been. There are missing people every day. It happens everywhere all the time. How do we know who is an actual missing person and who was taken by the manticore?" she asked. "We don't know. It just doesn't make any sense. But I need to figure out where it is. People dying is bad enough, but I need to find it so that nobody else does. I can't let him get it, Linx. He's made me question whether or not I want to work with him anymore. This is bad."

"Why is this bad?" Linx asked.

Haydeez shook her head. "I don't think I can do this anymore. I mean, how am I supposed to do this job for him when I question his motives for every single job he pays me for? Should I even care? Why does this matter so much to me?" She groaned.

Linx shrugged. "It matters to you because you don't want to see that creature roaming around under some crazy man's control. He's not exactly normal, is he? Normal people don't want to own killer animals. This thing is beyond a killer. It has no business being out there, and he wants to own it. You can't own chaos," he said. "If you choose to stay away from him, I'm behind you all the way. If you want to continue to work for him, well, I may just have to leave," he joked.

Haydeez chuckled. "I'm serious. I don't know what to do. If I stop working for him, I won't know what he's doing. But if I continue to work for him, I have to give him what he wants. Either way, something bad could happen and it would be my fault."

"It's not your fault that he's crazy," Linx said quickly. "He will find a way to get what he wants whether you answer the call or not. And there are probably many other people out there willing to give him what he wants. Might not be a bad idea to stay close. That way you will always know what it is that he's after. Besides, if he starts letting those things back out into the world, you can charge him double for having to do it all again."

"Stop it. I'm trying to be serious here," Haydeez said. "Obviously I'm sticking around for right now until all this Pandora garbage is over. I need to keep my focus so I don't screw up. Although it doesn't really matter because I'm not exactly the one who has to lock Pandora away." She sighed. "I'm so stressed right now. This is just all so screwed up."

Linx sighed and moved the laptop away from himself. "Look, it's not screwed up. *He's* screwed up. Honestly, if we didn't see something like this coming from him, we're both a little stupid," he said. "Let's be honest with ourselves. He treats you like you're a stray dog. He talks down to you all the time. The only good thing about him is his money. Right now, this is probably the least screwed up we've been in a long time. We have an answer to the Pandora issue. There's an end in sight, love. We now know what Peter wants from you and it's not just your pretty face," he joked.

"Ha ha, you're so funny," Haydeez scoffed.

Linx cleared his throat. "I know. I'm willing to bet that you at least smiled though," he said with a smirk. "We know where he stands and it's not on our side. So, we stick around. We do the jobs. We work with him for now. When it becomes too much, we deal with him. Until then, you collect all the paychecks you can."

Haydeez sighed. "I guess. I don't know why he's getting under my skin so much lately. There's always been a love-hate thing with us. But recently, it's like every time I talk to him, I just want to reach through the phone and punch him in the face. He just makes me so mad for some reason. It's like when they overplay a song on the radio. At first it's ok, but then you hear it one too many times and it just makes you want to kill everyone singing it."

Linx chuckled. "Well, that went dark very quickly. The sad thing is that I know what you're talking about," he said. "Sometimes, you put up with the little things because, in the end, it's worth it. But when those little things add up, they start to tip the scales and it finally pushes you over the edge."

"Exactly! See, this is why I keep you around," she said. "You understand me."

Linx nodded. "More than you know, love." He sighed. "So, how are we going to find this manticore? I know that Peter told you the last place it was seen. Did he tell you how long ago that happened?"

She shook her head. "He's never very clear with this kind of stuff. He'll give me a general idea and, if I'm lucky, he might know how to kill it." She paused. "I have not been very lucky."

Linx laughed. "I wouldn't say that. You've been pretty successful over the years. Most people would have died long before now if they had tried to do even half the stuff you've lived through. I would say that's pretty lucky."

"That, my friend, is skill, not luck," she joked. "Have you found a pattern yet? More missing people than usual in an area? I really need something to go on."

Linx picked up the laptop. "Right now, I'm not really sure if this is right. I'm seeing a small increase in some areas. I don't know how much this thing eats, so I don't know if this is too much or maybe too little to be the creature," he said. "All I know is that it's an increase. It's the only thing we have to go on right now. I would try the last place it was and see if you can scan the area for any kind of trace energies. If it gives off anything, we might be able to track it that way."

"It has a smell," Ra said calmly. "You will know it by its smell. It is a distinct odor of trees and rotting flesh. If you smell it, you will know that the beast has been there." He never turned from the window.

Linx furrowed his brow and said, "And you're just now sharing this with us?"

Ra glanced behind himself and said, "My apologies, child. As my strength increases, my mind and memories are returned to me. I have just regained a great deal recently with the aid of the young lady, Haydeez. She has been most gracious and helpful. With her assistance, my memories have been jump started. This will be a wonderful benefit when it comes to entrap Pandora." He watched the people outside like a child. He smiled and giggled as they casually walked around and went about their business. None of them knew that a god watched their movements and heard their silent prayers. While there were not many, his followers were still out there and he could feel them, all of them. "Hello, my children. I am sorry to be gone for so long," he mumbled. "But I have returned and I will make it all up to you soon. You will once again know your god."

Linx shook his head. "It's getting a little weird over here, love. Are you sure I can't join you. I mean, I'll even walk to where you are right now. I don't know how to take this," he whispered. "He's talking to the people outside and just watching them like a creepy stalker man."

Haydeez chuckled. "Nope. You're stuck there because I need you to keep looking. Plus, someone needs to babysit our weird friend there. Thanks for taking one for the team," she said with a laugh. "You're a real team player."

"That's just not right, love. I do so much for you and this is what I get in return?" Linx said. "That's just wrong." He pulled up another missing person report. Attached was a witness statement. "Hey, when there's a missing person, there's usually not a witness right?" he asked.

She shook her head. "Not that I know of. Usually 'missing' means nobody saw where they went or if they were kidnapped or whatever. It means they just went away and nobody knows anything. Why do you ask?"

He cocked his head to the side and read the screen. "Well, this one had a witness statement. It says the witness saw a large shadowy figure pick up the person and eat it. It looks like there were two different reports made and they ended up matching the statement with the description of a missing person." He checked the date. "This report just came in. Wait, we're going about this all wrong. You have to wait at least twenty four hours to file a missing person's report. These stats aren't going to help us at all. Any report filed would have to be no less than a day ago. How is that going to help? We don't know how long ago she let it out." He straightened up on the bed. "We really have nothing to go on but the information that Ra gave us."

"The manticore smells of the forest and rotten eggs. The mixture is quite rancid and potent. You will definitely be able to tell that it is there,"

Ra mused. "He will try to hide and give the impression of being an old man to lure people to their deaths. He will appear to be frail and in need of assistance. You must be weary as he will strike hard and fast. The manticore devours everything you have with you. Nothing will be left behind for anyone to find. It will be as if you were never there."

"Well, aren't you just a brand new fount of information," Linx mumbled. "Did you catch all that?" he asked Haydeez.

"Yup, but how do I use the ivory? If this thing is like the Chimera, it'll be hard to kill," she said. "I had to fire that arrow straight into the fire to get it in his mouth. Please tell me this is going to be easier."

Linx laughed. "Is it ever?"

Ra smiled at the people again. "The jaw is most vulnerable. The hide is too thick to pierce with the ivory. You must strike it in the jaw."

Haydeez sighed. "Great. Hit the mouth again. Awesome. At least this one doesn't shoot fire at me while I'm trying to kill it. I guess that's a positive."

"No, there is no fire but you must be weary of the spikes. He will try to impale you by firing large spikes from his tail. If he fires one, a new one will take its place. They regenerate on their own," Ra said. "You must watch what the tail is doing as he will try to distract you with his face and quickly strike with the tail. He is a skilled hunter and does not lose often. Only a few have ever bested him in battle."

"Well, that's pleasant," Haydeez scoffed. "Any more little fun facts you'd like to share with me? Does it shoot lasers from its eyes? Does it bring trees to life? Hmm, anything else?" she asked.

Ra cocked his head to the side. "Lasers from his eyes? Not at all, child. His eyes are quite normal, I assure you of that. I have never seen a creature that can command nature either. You are safe from that as well," he answered.

Haydeez groaned. "He's beginning to get on my nerves. I'm glad he's stuck with you."

"I'll try to teach him sarcasm before you get back," Linx joked. "Ok, so, back to finding the manticore. Are you at the place he said to go?"

"Yup," she answered.

"Have you checked it out yet?"

"Nope, been talking to you guys since I pulled up."

"Ok, so go check it out. See if you can smell it out there." Linx chuckled. "Maybe you can track his scent."

"Woof, woof. That means 'watch it or I'll make you sleep in the sand outside the hotel tonight'," she said. "I would've gotten out sooner but you just kept talking and if I don't give you my undivided attention, you get cranky." She opened the door and immediately regretted it. "Ugh, that's awful. Is that what these things smell like? No wonder nothing gets close enough to take it out. It's making me want to throw up and it's not even around." She waved in front of her face but there was no escape from the stench. "It smells like burnt trees and eggs that went bad and baked in the sun for a week. Normally I can stand either smell on its own, but for some reason the two together is just so much worse. I don't know what I was expecting but apparently I wasn't ready for this."

Ra nodded. "Then you have found where he has been. If the scent is still that strong, he has not been gone for too long. If you follow the smell, it gets stronger when you are close, child. Look for an old man in need of help. That is how he traps his victims. That is when you will need to watch for the spikes. He will be quick. You will need to be quicker."

Haydeez rolled her neck and breathed through her mouth. She reached back into the car and pulled out the tusk. As she looked around, the silence caught her off guard. "Why is it so quiet here? This is a city and I don't see people or hear cars or anything. I mean, it's late in the day but there would still be something going on here at this hour. Does that seem weird to anyone?" she asked.

"What do you mean? Like there's literally nobody there?" Linx asked.

Haydeez scanned the area again. "Right, there's nobody here. I don't even see people in the windows or walking in the distance. I don't see anybody. I'm right on the river and there's nothing. Why wouldn't there be anyone here?"

"He will take a single person if there is nothing else. However, he prefers to take groups of people as it is more of a challenge for him," Ra said calmly. "Perhaps everyone there was taken. It is possible as his hunger is rarely satiated. He will continue to hunt until there is nothing more to hunt or someone stops him. You will need to stop him. There is no other option, child."

She scoffed. "Well that just ruined my plans. I was going to let it go free." She paused and looked around again. "Don't talk for a minute," she whispered and sniffed the air. Her eyes scanned the area slowly. There was a light breeze that came off the river and gave her a slight reprieve from the foul odor that accosted her nostrils. "I heard something just now. I think it's still here." She stood completely still except for her head as she looked through the trees and the tall grass along the water. She took a few slow, tentative steps forward. "Oh wow, that has to be it," she said. "It's just sitting there, waiting. How long do they usually wait?"

"They will hide for as long as it takes. They may never move from an area if there is enough to hunt," Ra answered. "He may have found a home for himself. He will be more aggressive to protect it now. Be watchful of his movements. As soon as he sees the weapon, he will become angry and protective."

"It won't have a chance to protect anything. I'm going to take it out and get this over with. I'm getting a little tired of all these things just showing up everywhere. I'm tired of Pandora and her little tirade to get daddy's attention. I've had enough," she growled. "This thing has to know I'm here. No point in hiding myself. If I can smell you, you can probably smell me too." She stood up straight and held the tusk tight in her hand. "Come on out, you filthy animal. I know you're here. I'm sure you want to eat me, although I'm a little small and more of a snack than a full meal. I want a fight. Come and get me," she yelled. "I'm right here. I'm in your new home. Let's go!"

A tree shifted under the weight of the creature and dropped leaves onto the ground. There was a low growl and the creak of the branches. The creature opened its mouth and a soft song began to play. It moved its jaws like it tried to speak but the sound of a trumpet was all that came out. The creature cocked its head and moved back and forth as it locked eyes with Haydeez. It had crystal blue eyes that were so pale, they were a few shades from white. The face resembled a man with a full beard and a large jawline. The beard connected to the long hair that flowed down over its shoulders. It perched on a branch with its wings tucked behind its back and 'spoke' to Haydeez.

"Why is it singing to me?" she asked.

"Singing?" Linx asked.

"That is how he communicates, child. He speaks in song when he is preparing to hunt," Ra answered. "If you hear his song, he is going to attack soon. If there is no prey nearby, he will lure victims into the forest with his song."

"The manticore is making music?" Linx asked. "Like a siren?"

"Yup," Haydeez said. "Wow, if I didn't have to kill you, buddy," she added. She watched as it swayed slowly back and forth to its own music. The creature's mouth looked awkward as it tried to move like a human's mouth. "I've never seen anything like you before," she mumbled. "Linx, I'll call you back when I'm done." She clicked off her phone before he could answer her, and stuffed it in her pocket. "You are just an amazing creature aren't you?" she said as she slowly walked towards the tree. "You're not going to hurt me are you? You don't want to flick those nasty spikes at me, right?" She hid the tusk behind her back.

The creature cocked its head to the side and continued its song. It locked eyes with Haydeez and watched every move she made. With a sniff, its nose moved through the air. The branch creaked as the creature crouched down. It swung its tail beneath the branch and its muscles bunched as it prepared to leap down.

"Coming down to see me up close? Good because I can't reach you up on that branch," Haydeez mumbled. "It's weird to fight something that doesn't talk to back to me. Doesn't happen too often." She stopped and steadied herself.

In a burst of fur and tail spikes, the creature leapt down to the ground and landed with a thump and a growl. It began to pace back and forth like a tiger trapped in a cage. The tip of its tail twitched in anticipation. Its large, scaled wings spread wide behind its body. The creature flexed its claws and dug into the ground. Clumps of grass and dirt turned over after each step. It never broke eye contact with Haydeez and never turned its back on her.

"So, here we are. I guess it's too much to ask for you to just lie down and take the hit from me, right?" she joked. "Not that you can answer me anyway." She stood still, only her eyes moved along with the manticore's movements. "So, how long do we do this dance before you come after me?" she asked. Her eyes were so stuck on the creature's face that she almost did not see its tail disappear behind the wings and then reappear above its head.

Long spikes flew through the air straight for her heart.

Haydeez dropped to the ground and rolled to the side. One of the spikes brushed past her hair and pulled a few strands out. "What the hell!" she yelled. "Oh that's just so not cool. We are not friends anymore! Friends don't try to kill each other with long spikes. And yes, I realize the hypocrisy as I stand here with an ivory tusk in my hand waiting to stab you," she added.

The creature began its song again.

"Oh, so that's what you do. You sing to me to distract me. That way I won't see those nasty spikes coming at my head. Sneaky little booger," she said. "Tricky tricky, but now that I know what you're doing," she paused and gripped the tusk tight. "I'm not going to fall for it anymore. That was a pretty nifty trick you did but fool me twice..." She crouched down and prepared for the next strike.

The creature flicked its tail again and sent another set of spikes at her. She jumped to the side and ran forward. She struck out just as the manticore snapped its jaws at her. The tusk missed its mark. "Damn it!" she yelled and pulled back. She stepped back out of reach and watched the creature pace again. "You must rely entirely on those spikes to stop your prey."

It swatted at her with a giant clawed paw. The calm song that called the prey closer changed. It sounded as if the creature was angry now. Its eyes narrowed. Each step was now more of a stomp instead of the quiet footfalls when it first started. The creature snapped its jaws and slammed its paw down. It let out a bellowing trumpet sound and flicked more spikes at her.

She jumped out of the way as one spike grazed her shoulder. "Damn it!" she yelled again. "That actually hurt." She straightened up and touched the scrape. Small speckles of blood covered her fingers. "That means you ripped my shirt. I liked this shirt. You suck." She rolled her shoulders and touched the wound once more. "I really don't like you now. I was seriously considering letting you live but not anymore, jerk." She wiped the blood on her pants and adjusted her grip on the tusk. "I'm going to jam this right into your mouth." She did not wait for the creature to attack this time. With her knees bent, she ran forward and pounced at the manticore.

The creature cocked its head in surprise. It quickly tried to compensate and flicked its tail but the spikes landed behind Haydeez. They thumped into the ground and completely missed their mark. It now had to wait for new spikes to emerge before it could throw more.

Haydeez jumped up to reach the creature's face. She held the tusk with the point flat against her wrist and swiped backwards.

The ivory tusk struck the creature's jawbone and it howled in pain. Her hand vibrated with the force of the strike. The manticore flung its head from side to side but the ivory remained embedded into the bone. The trumpet sound was now a more urgent blast. The intensity increased the more the creature flailed. Blood sprayed everywhere. It coated the pure white elephant tusk. Haydeez had managed to slam the ivory right into the hinge of the jaw.

It could not close its jaws anymore. The more it tried to bite down, the more pain it was in and the more blood that spilled out. It feebly reached up with a paw and tried to pull the projectile from its face. It scraped at the ivory but only managed to spill more blood. It tried to open its mouth wide and snap down. The force used to close its jaw caused the hinge to break and left the creature with a broken jaw. It slumped to the ground as the bottom teeth just hung there, limp and useless. The creature tried to trumpet a sad song but began to choke on its own blood.

Haydeez walked over slowly. She cocked her head to the side and looked at the ivory tusk as it protruded from the creature's face. With all her strength, she yanked it free and, without another thought, she jammed it a little further back. She pushed hard to make sure it went as far in as possible. "Sorry. You really were an interesting creature, but I couldn't let you live. You're just too dangerous and there's no way I was going to put you into the hands of a crazy man. You just don't belong in this world," she said and pushed again.

The creature groaned and twitched. It fell over onto its side. The dragon-like wings flopped down onto the ground with a smack. Its eyes rolled back into its head and glazed over.

She bent down and yanked the ivory tusk from the creature's lifeless face. "Not going to just leave this sitting here. I bet it cost a lot to get this on such short notice. Don't want to have to get one again if I need it later, not that you'll be visiting us again," she said to the creature. "I'm sorry your life had to be sacrificed to Pandora. I bet you had no idea what she's up to. You probably didn't even want to be let out. But here you are, dead, because that little psycho wants to kill everyone on the planet. I actually feel sorry for you. You guys were all just pawns for her to get what she wanted." She leaned over and wiped the blood in the grass. "And now she's probably going to just suck the life out of you and gain even more strength from it. You're a killer, that's true, but you don't deserve to be used like that." She stood up. "I'm sorry. I'm going to find her and stop her now."

As she turned to walk away, the creature's body had just started to flatten out. Haydeez did not even need to look for the symbol. She knew where this creature had come from and what would happen to it after she left. Pandora needed energy and she would do whatever she could to get it. That part was inevitable. She could not stop that. What she *could* stop was the end of the human race. She sniffed to clear out her nostrils of the stench and continued to walk back to the car.

• • •

"Ugh, I really hate when she does that," Linx groaned. "When you agree to stay in contact with someone, why do you insist on hanging up on them?"

Ra smiled at Linx. "Am I to assume that she does this frequently?"

Linx nodded.

"Then perhaps you should be comfortable now with the way that things work, child. I would ask if you trust her but I can see that there is a great deal of trust within your relationship," Ra said.

"We're not in a relationship," Linx blurted.

"Are you not friends?" Ra asked.

"Oh, well, yes, of course we're friends. I guess that counts as a relationship then," Linx said as he fumbled over his words. "I just thought you meant... never mind." He turned back to the laptop and began to type again.

The room was silent for several minutes. The only sound was the occasional click of the keyboard.

Then, Linx looked up and asked, "What is the *Cave of Zeus?*"

Ra turned back to him. "That would be the sacred birthplace of Zeus. It is said that when Zeus was born, his father, Kronos, wanted to eat him as he usually did with all of his children. I was not yet born myself at that time, so I am not aware of the validity of that claim. However, that is the legend of his birth. His mother gave life to him on that island and hid him from his father for many years," Ra answered.

"Hmm, so they were able to hide there for a long time and nobody knew he was there," Linx said. "So, someone had to help her hide there. What if whoever helped her hide there with Zeus also helped Pandora hide there with her children? Is that possible?" Linx asked.

Ra nodded. "It is possible. There has always been plenty of deception within the Greek pantheon. For some reason they had a great deal of anger and hatred when it came to their children. It was as if they were afraid someone else would attempt to destroy them and take over in their stead. Unfortunately, most of them were right to be afraid, as their children did ultimately destroy them and take over. The Titans came first. Kronos was the father of the Titans." He sighed. "When you base everything on a claim of power, your existence is fraught with peril and anger. I have spoken those words so many times to my own children. While some do listen, others just ignore and continue down that dangerous path. One day, I had hoped to be able to pass my mantel on to one of my own children, but it appears that will never happen."

Linx turned the laptop around. "Is this the actual place? Do you know if this is actually where he was born?"

Ra turned to the screen. "I have not seen the cave in person, but I do believe that the location is correct. They hid him there until he was old enough to take on his father and remove him from his throne. They have held that as a sacred place since his birth."

"So, Pandora would know about this place. She could use it to hide her kids as well. She could be there now!" Linx said excitedly. "What if this is where she is? Is it possible that we found her?" he asked.

Ra nodded slowly. "I could see it being a place of great power. It is possible that she hid his children there, the same way he was hidden from his father in that cave. It would make a great deal of sense," Ra answered.

Linx grabbed the phone and started to dial. He stopped and said, "Wait, if she's in the middle of a fight, she won't answer. I'll have to wait until she calls me. Well, that's just anticlimactic. I guess we just sit here and wait then. Any other little tidbits of god knowledge that you would like to share with me today?" Linx joked as he set the laptop aside and leaned back on the bed. "I love a good story."

Chapter 25

Pandora gloated. "She has killed the manticore! I knew that she would. She has proven more than capable of defeating these insipid creatures. Powerful as they are, they truly do not serve another purpose. I have gained what I need from them and now I am able to move forward with my plans. Once your brother finally arrives, we will be ready to finish this," she said to Pyrrha. "It won't be long now, my daughter. Your father wanted me to do this one day. He made sure that I would be able to kill you and I am happy to take on that responsibility." She bent down and stroked Pyrrha's hair. The gentle motherly act became twisted and demented when Pandora looked down at the woman who cowered near the fire. "You have nothing to worry about anymore. Everything will be over soon," she cooed. "I will ensure that it is quick. One moment you will be here and the next, it will all be over. You will not feel pain any longer after that because you will no longer exist. Even your spirit will be gone. Everything will be as it should be and I will have fulfilled my purpose." She smiled.

"Who killed a manticore? Am I hallucinating now?" Pyrrha asked. "Is that how far gone I am now?"

Pandora giggled. "No, my child. I unleashed a manticore on the earth and my adversary has killed it. She gave me all the power within the creature and now I am strong enough to complete my task. You should be proud. Your mother is finally ready to become everything that she was created for all those years ago. My entire existence has been for this moment, my child. Are you happy for me?" she asked.

Pyrrha furrowed her filthy brow. "Proud?" she coughed. "Proud that you want to destroy the world? Why would that make anyone proud? You want to kill me to complete some psychotic purpose that you think you have. You keep saying I'm your daughter but we've never met. I don't know who you are." She tried to take a deep breath but it was more of a wheeze. "No, I'm not proud that you get to kill me. That's just insane." She coughed again and slumped back down to the ground.

Pandora smiled. "There are no worries now, my child. I know that you will be proud of me when the time comes to take your life. You and your brother will know greatness at that moment. You will know what it is like to be more than what you see in the mirror," she said and stood up. "Now, to find out where he is, because I am tired of waiting for him." She walked over to the egg and brushed her fingertips over the outside.

The heat that pulsed from the egg was almost enough to put the fire to shame. It hummed and vibrated with its own inner energy. She put her palms flat on the shell and closed her eyes.

Images of a man flashed in her head. He sat on a train. The countryside flew past in a blur as he slept silently in his seat.

"I see you, my son. I finally see you and you are not far from me," she whispered. "We will all be together again soon. Our family will finally be whole again, if only for a moment. You will know your mother and sister, and then, you will know greatness as I take your life and destroy the human race." She giggled. "Hurry home, my son." She opened her eyes and placed the egg gently on the floor. A shiver danced up her body and she chuckled. "Hurry home."

Chapter 26

"It's dead. Put the money in my account," Haydeez said.

"No hello for your friend?" Peter asked.

"I would say hello if I was talking to a friend," she answered.

"I'm sad you don't consider me a friend. That's just too bad, Ms. Blackhawk," Peter said. "I always pictured us taking on the world together. I guess that will never happen now that I know how you really feel about me."

Haydeez cleared her throat. "I thought I made it clear how I felt before. I'm not interested in your games. We have a working agreement, and I will not give you something that you can use as a weapon. It's that simple, Peter. I'm not required to tell you anything and you pay me when the job is done. That's how we work. If we deviate from that, our relationship breaks down and things get screwed up. Let's not mess it up by adding in unnecessary elements," she said. "I tried to be pleasant but apparently we're beyond that. So, for now we keep things civil and this will work. When the time comes that we can't be civil anymore, we'll part ways and never have to deal with each other again. How does that sound?" she asked.

Peter sighed. "Well, Ms. Blackhawk, your money has been taken care of and we will be in touch when you're needed again," Peter said and ended the call without another word.

Haydeez placed her phone on the seat next to her, wrapped her fingers tightly around the steering wheel, and yelled. No actual words came out. It was mostly grunts and screams. She let out one last groan and sighed heavily. "Ok, I'm ok. I can drive now," she said with another sigh. "I'm better." She turned on the car and shifted into gear.

As she drove down the road, she said, "Oh shoot," and grabbed her phone. "Hey, it's me. I'm done and I'm on my way back." She glanced down at her shirt and all the blood splatter. "I had to cover the seat first before I sat down. Didn't want to drip blood on the rental. It got pretty gross. I mean, come on, you had to know that was going to happen. I stabbed it in the jaw. There was bound to be blood and crud," she joked.

Linx sighed. "But the tusk worked then, right?" he asked.

"Yup, it's dead. Pandora got her mystical mojo and now she's stronger and we have no idea where she is," she said with another sigh. "I feel like we're just spinning our wheels here. We have nothing to go on and we're no closer to stopping her than we were when we first found out what was going on."

"I wouldn't say that. I mean, we have the way to stop her," Linx said. "Not to mention I think we may have figured out where she is. Did I forget to tell you that?" he joked.

She scoffed. "Seriously? Why didn't you call me?"

Linx chuckled. "I didn't know if you were busy. Didn't want to bother you in the middle of one of your fierce battles and all that. Besides, we just found it a few minutes ago. Want to hear about it?"

"Of course. Where are we going?" she asked.

"There's a large island in the Mediterranean Sea that has a cave on it called, get this, 'Zeus's Cave'," he answered excitedly. "Ra says it's where Zeus was born and kept hidden from Kronos so he wouldn't eat him and all that. Weird huh? But anyway, we think that Pandora did the same thing with her kids when she was pregnant. We think the same person that helped Zeus's mother was the one that showed Pandora the cave, and she went there to give birth. How appropriate to hide his children from him in the same place that he was born and hidden from his father. It's just so poetic. What do you think?" he asked.

Haydeez nodded. "I think it sounds good. Might want to let the others know we're heading out and get us checked out," she said.

"Already started packing," Linx answered.

•   •   •

"So, do you want us to come too?" Checkmate asked. "You might need help."

Haydeez shook her head. "I would prefer if we had as few people as possible there. I have no idea what will happen with this spell of his, or what Pandora is planning to do. I don't want anyone else to get hurt in all of this. We're going to end this. I can't stop you from going, but I also don't have to take you with me. It's nothing against you in particular. You've proven that you're more than capable of dealing with this stuff, but I can't put anyone else in danger," she said.

Night Raven nodded. "It would probably be best if we take a moment to rest. We will take care of everything here and then meet back up with you when we are done," he said calmly. "Are you sure that you have everything you need to end this?"

Haydeez nodded. "We don't need anything but him," she said and motioned to Ra who stood with his back to the window now. "Are you ready to do this?" she asked Ra.

Ra just smiled and motioned to the door.

"I'll take that as a 'yes'. Alright then. Let's go to Greece."

●　　　●　　　●

Haydeez powered down the highway towards the center of the island of Crete. Her eyes remained on the road. She felt the end near and nothing would deter her. She turned off the main road and headed west. She glanced at the clock. "How long before we get there?" she asked.

"Around three hours," Linx said as he checked the GPS. "Then again, that depends on how determined you are," he joked.

Haydeez shook her head. "Too many winding roads around here. I don't want to get this close and lose because we fell off the side of a mountain," she said. "Maybe on the way back," she added with a smirk.

Linx lifted his head and asked, "Wait, did we leave Ra on the plane?"

"Shut up, punk," she said. "I would kill you if you left him back at the airfield, because that was the only thing I left you in charge of." She glanced at him. "That would be your fault. Are you alright back there?" she asked. "You don't get car sick or anything do you? I probably should've asked that long before now but it didn't even cross my mind until this moment."

Ra chuckled. "I used to travel across the heavens daily. I do not get ill. It is one of many perks of being a god, my child. Our bodies do not have imperfections like those that plague humans daily. My apologies to both of you if you are afflicted with illnesses," he answered.

Haydeez sighed. "Lucky us, I guess. Thankfully, carsick is not one of my problems. Airsick I get, but not car or boat," she said. "So, is there anything we need to do for this spell? I know you have to be the one to actually say it, because you have all the power and stuff. But, do we need to do anything?"

Ra shook his head. "I do not require any assistance from you. I do ask that you make sure that any humans are not right next to her when I recite the spell," he said. "I have never done this before and I am unsure of the ramifications. There could be reverberations that may harm one of you. I could not protect you while I am in the middle of the incantation."

"So, that's all we're supposed to do while you're doing all this?" Linx asked.

"Yes, keep the humans away from her and remove the egg," Ra answered. "And then leave the cave as quickly as you can. You will need to be away from her as well, child. You are not human." He looked at Haydeez. "I am not sure what you are though. I can see something but it is behind a cloud as if someone has hidden it. Do you hide what you are?" he asked.

"Excuse me?" Haydeez scoffed. "I'm human too. What else could I be? You might be seeing the brands that my father put on me when I was little. They're probably clouding your sight."

Ra smiled. "You are probably correct. I must be mistaken. My apologies, my child."

Haydeez furrowed her brow. "I'm getting tired of people saying I'm not a human. I mean, look at me. Do I not look human enough for everyone?" she asked angrily.

"Maybe you're just too perfect for everyone to believe it," Linx joked.

She shot him an irritated glance. "Not helping."

"True, but it's still funny. Come on, you know what you are, love. Who cares what other people say? They do it just to get under your skin," he said. "Don't let them bother you."

"I hate when people say stuff like that, like I can just turn off my irritation. It's not a switch and I'm not building a bridge to get over it. Have we covered all the annoying sayings yet?" she asked. "How much longer?"

"Still a little under three hours," Linx answered. "This is going to be a long three hours isn't it?"

"We'll park here. I don't want to get too close so she sees us coming. Don't leave anything in the car. We need to be quick about this. We don't know if both kids are in there yet or what she's already done to them," Haydeez said. She looked ahead to the path up the mountain. "Do you get cold at all? I never even thought to ask."

Ra shook his head. "Not at all. My body holds the world's light. I am always warm," he answered.

"Well, that's handy. Ok, so, the cave is closed to the public right now because of the season. So, we don't have to worry about a bunch of tourists getting in the way. That means we only need to rescue the kids, grab the egg, and put Pandora away. Sounds easy enough, right."

Linx chuckled. "Sure, easy. Should be a walk in the park..." he paused. "A snowy, icy park up the side of a mountain in a cave where death is waiting for us." He clapped his hands together and added, "So, let's get started, right?"

Haydeez grabbed her duffel bag. She had replaced most of her weapons with blankets and a medic kit in case the kids needed medical attention. She knew she would not need to fight as much as take care of people, but she still brought one weapon. The stone dagger from Cornelius sat quietly in its box. It waited for the moment she would need to take it out and use it again. She could feel its presence. The weight of it was an awkward comfort to her. She was not sure how to feel about it right now. While she did not like the feeling it gave her and how it took control of her body, she did enjoy the results she got from it. She had decided that it was merely there as an emergency assistance. Until the world depended on it, that dagger would sit silently in the bottom of her bag.

The trio quietly closed the doors and began their hike up the mountain. Fresh snow covered the peak and cascaded down the side. Linx zipped his jacket up to his chin and pulled the hood over his head. He walked close to Haydeez and leaned towards her. "Is it wrong for me to be nervous about this?" he asked.

She shook her head. "Don't worry. I won't make fun of you later," she said with a smile. She bumped him with her shoulder as they continued to walk.

Ra frowned slightly. "I can hear a prayer," he said. "It is a woman. She is terrified and alone. I can hear her but she is not praying to me. I cannot answer her."

Haydeez looked at Ra. "You can't tell her she'll be ok or that we're coming to save her?"

He shook his head. "Unless she prays directly to me, I cannot. I am sorry."

She sighed. "Ok, let's get going before it's too late."

The winds picked up the higher they went. Ice and snow covered every inch of the mountain and made the journey treacherous. Haydeez gripped the side of the mountain as she climbed, but her gloved fingers slipped and she fell forward to her knee. Linx grabbed her arm. She leaned close to him and said, "Watch that spot. There's ice on the wall. I can't get a good grip with these gloves on."

Linx nodded and helped her up.

By the time they reached the mouth of the cave, the winds whipped around them and threatened to throw them from the cliffs. Linx and Haydeez hugged the wall, but Ra seemed to be able to stand without an issue. His body appeared to hover above the ground as well.

"Seriously?" Haydeez mumbled to the wind. Her body shivered involuntarily as she slid along the wall. "We have to get inside! Now!" she yelled but her words were cut off by the storm.

Linx pressed his hand against her back and hugged the wall with the other. He nodded and followed her into the mouth of darkness.

Ra moved without making a sound, as if his body was a mere image and not the flesh and blood that was actually there. His head cocked to the side, and he whispered, "She is inside. I feel her energy."

Haydeez nodded toward the soft light further down the tunnel. She moved through the tunnel, careful not to bump a rock. Her shoes slid along the ground without a scrape.

The soft flicker became a warm glow and flooded the end of the tunnel. Haydeez crouched down and poked her head around the corner. She held back a gasp as her eyes fell on the figure in the middle of the cave.

Black curly hair billowed around the woman's pale face. Her eyes remained closed as she whispered.

Haydeez could not understand the words. As she pulled herself back behind the rocks, she turned to her companions and mouthed, "Pandora".

Linx let out a quiet sigh. "Is she alone?" he asked, his voice barely above a whisper.

Haydeez held up a finger and moved to sneak another peek. She scanned the cavern slowly. Her brow furrowed. If someone else was in there, she could not see them.

Just as she moved to slip back behind the rocks, a small, almost unnoticeable movement, caught her eye. A hand reached out from around the curve in the path. There was a soft groan followed by a whimper. Haydeez glanced at Pandora, and back to the hand. Pandora did not notice the noise or the movement. Haydeez motioned for Linx to come up to her. She pointed to the limp limb.

Linx nodded. He pointed to himself as if to ask if he should make his way over there.

Haydeez shook her head. "Not yet," she mouthed and pulled him back. She turned to Ra and asked, "What do we need to do?"

Ra stood quietly. He took a deep breath and let it out slowly. "Do you feel that?" he asked. "Her power is growing. The final piece is almost here. She will need it before she can kill her children."

"What's the final piece?" Linx asked.

"Her son," Ra answered as he opened his eyes. "He is near. We must push her back into her prison before she kills him."

Haydeez looked at Linx. "Ok, now you can get her."

Linx nodded.

Haydeez moved into view and picked up a rock. She hurled it at Pandora with a grunt.

Linx raced out from where they hid towards the spot where the hand sat quietly on the ground.

As the rock struck Pandora, she spun around. Her eyes sprung open. There was nothing but darkness where her pupils had been. The black abyss spread out and bled into the whites of her eyes.

"Oops," Haydeez said. "I guess I didn't see you hovering there." She waved. "But since I have your attention now, how have you been? It's been a while since we chatted. I see you've grown up a bit." She bent down to pick up another rock. "So, what's new?"

Pandora growled. "You are not my child. You can leave now," she said and turned back around.

"Nah, I think I'll stick around for now," Haydeez said. Her eyes shot quickly towards Linx and then back to Pandora.

Linx had his arms around a woman who was slumped on the floor. He leaned and tried to drag her. Linx turned his gaze back to Haydeez, frustration apparent on his face. "Come on, dear. You have to work with me," he whispered.

"Won't let go," the woman breathed.

"What's that? What won't let go?" Linx asked.

She tried to shake her head but only managed to flop down on his leg. "She... she won't," the woman was finally able to say. Her fingers trembled as she moved her hand to point.

Linx turned towards Pandora and sighed. "We won't let her keep you here," he said and began to pull her again.

Haydeez glanced back and forth between Linx and Pandora again and then looked down at the rock in her hand. "So, I see you're missing stuff. Are you sure you're ready to finish this?" She threw the rock at Pandora.

It smacked into Pandora's back with a thump. She spun quickly and glared at Haydeez. "Gnat! We could have been sisters. I tried to make you understand. You will see! When my task is complete, you will be alone. You deserve to be alone. Your existence is an abomination!" she yelled.

A warm gust of wind swirled around Pandora. Pebbles trembled at her feet.

Haydeez cocked her head to the side. "Are you going to fight me? Is that what's about to happen?" she asked. "You have been both a pain and a boon the last few months. While I appreciate the money you've added to my account because Peter can't handle your creatures roaming around, it's the other stuff I can't allow." She bent down to pick up another rock. "Because of you, too many people have died or been seriously hurt. I'm not letting you leave here tonight. I'm not letting you finish what you started." She pulled her arm back, prepared to toss the rock in her hand. "And no, we could never be sisters. Whatever you think I am, you're wrong. I don't know what's going on in that psycho brain of yours, but I'm just me.

Whatever you are, we're not family. We're enemies and I will stop you." She tossed the rock and began to move further into the cavern. "No matter what happens to me, you lose." She took off at a sprint and circled the pool.

In spite of the wind around Pandora, the waters remained oddly calm. It was as if they did not realize that there was a storm in the cave. The black glassy liquid hid an eternity of history beneath its depths.

Haydeez glanced at the water and noticed that, while is shimmered, there was no reflection on the surface. It was as if the night sky had liquefied and filled the pool. Her brow furrowed.

Pandora stood completely still, eyes closed. She mumbled to herself, "I feel you getting closer, my son. It is almost time." The winds began to swirl faster. A wave of warmth crept away from her body towards Haydeez.

As she reached the inside coil of the path, Haydeez stopped. The heat halted her like a wall and she stumbled back. She shook her head and glanced back to where Linx was hidden.

The woman groaned quietly, her voice barely above a whisper. Her head flopped back and forth slowly.

"Look, I'm going to need you to try. I can't lift you on my own. Right now, your body is like a dead weight," Linx whispered. "Please. I'm trying to save your life." He stuffed his arms under her arms and pulled. He managed to move her body a little, but it was not enough. They were still stuck behind a large boulder.

The flames from the small fire Pandora had built had started to die down. The shadows grew longer and fatter as they began to consume the light. While the glow faded, the heat remained. Pandora's energy had made its way around the pool and up to Linx.

Sweat formed on his forehead as he scooted along the stone and dirt. "Pretty soon she's going to see us and there's nothing I can do," he whispered. "You have to try." He pleaded with the woman. "You have to pull whatever strength you have left and drag yourself out of here. You're going to die if you don't. We're all going to die. We have to get out of this cave right now." He was on his side on the ground with her in front of his body as he used his legs to push across the dirt.

The woman wept. Her shoulders shook slightly. Dirt mixed with dried tears covered her face. Her body was so dehydrated that she no longer had tears. She tried to move her arms but her muscles seized. She clawed at the ground but her fingers froze. "Can't do it," she whimpered. The heat in the cave drew out any ounce of strength she had left. Her eyes rolled back into her head and her body went limp.

"Bollocks," Linx grunted as he felt her body collapse. "Well, if you're unconscious, at least you won't feel this." He stood up, grabbed her arms, and began to drag her. "I'm really sorry about this. It's not the way I wanted to do it."

Haydeez rushed forward into the wall of heat and pushed passed it. The air in her lungs became heavy. Her body looked as if she walked through water. Each step was large and slow. The air burned her throat but she finally made it in front of Pandora. She tried to take a swing but she felt like someone had dunked her in a thick, jelly-like substance. Her body moved in slow motion.

"Nothing you do matters now, child. This is the end. Now we will all see what you really are," Pandora said. She spoke softly but her voice echoed throughout the chamber. The golden disk glowed and pulsed in the middle of her chest. "In this cave, where human life began, you will see it all end." Her eyes flew open. They mirrored the dark pool behind her. "My son is near. Soon he will die along with his sister and man will cease to exist. The circle of life will be broken. How exciting it must be for you to be here for this event. When your life carries on, you will see. You will be revealed and your true self will no longer be hidden. Do not fight it, Haydeez. Embrace the end of man. Embrace your nature. Let their end be your new beginning!" Pandora opened her hands and moved them up in the air.

Haydeez shouted, "I'm just a human! Stop saying that! I don't know what you think I am, but I'm just me! Enough already!" The wind swirled her hair around her face. As she brushed the strands from her eyes, movement caught her gaze. The phenix egg floated through the air towards Pandora's waiting hands. "No!" Haydeez yelled. "I'm not letting you do this!"

Linx pulled the woman into the dark of the tunnel and moved back into the cave. "I've got her!" he shouted. "Grab it now!"

Pandora glanced up at Linx and back to Haydeez. "You cannot take the egg, child. Its power is too strong for you. Only I have the strength to touch it," she said with a smirk.

Haydeez pulled herself closer to Pandora. "It's not the egg I'm after, crazy lady," she said with a grunt. She could feel her body adjust to the pressure around her. Movements were easier and more fluid now. She smiled. "That egg won't stop you. I know that." Her eyes caught Pandora's as she pulled herself closer. The darkness of her irises pulled Haydeez in like an old friend. "There's only one way to stop you, Pandora. It's time to let the light in." Her hand moved quickly as she reached out to grab the glowing disk. With her eyes closed tight, she yanked down fast and snapped the chain in two.

A blinding light filled the cave. Pandora screamed in pain. The echoes shook the walls around them and reverberated back to her. She fell to her knees and clawed at her eyes in agony.

Haydeez stumbled back and reached around for the wall. She moved as quickly as she could along the outer edge. Even though her eyes had been closed, the light still caused colored bubbles to pop in her vision. She blinked multiple times in an attempt to clear it up as she ran. The dial was a blur but she had it. In her hand, Haydeez held Pandora's Box of evil.

"I've got you, love," Linx said. He grabbed her arm and pulled her into the tunnel. "I'll turn the dial, you say the incantation."

Haydeez nodded. She began to speak in a language older than Latin. Ra had taught her the exact words to say. Each syllable flowed from her lips with ease.

Linx spun each dial to the correct symbol in the exact order they had talked about earlier. He did not say a word. He made sure not to distract Haydeez.

The cloudy stone swirled and pulsed. It vibrated and shook his arms. As the last words slipped from her lips, a beam of green light shot from the center of the stone. Linx dropped the disk and pulled his hands back in pain. He looked down at a rounded burn mark in the palm of each hand.

Shadows spun and twisted out of the stone. They pulled themselves out and stretched into the darkness. Eyes glowed down the dark tunnel as the shadows made their way to the entrance.

"I hope we're doing the right thing," Haydeez mumbled.

Ra placed a glowing hand on her shoulder and said, "This is the only way, child. There is no other way."

A scream echoed down the tunnel. Haydeez and Linx turned to the darkness again. "That's not a good sign," Linx said.

"That's her son," Haydeez said. "We have to get them out of the cave."

Another scream echoed from inside the cavern. They turned to face the other direction. "I'm going to say that she's not happy right now," Haydeez said. "You have to do it now." She turned to Ra and handed him the disk.

He took the golden dials in his massive hand. In his palm, the disk resembled a coin. He had gained so much power that his body had grown again. The prayers and praise had continued even though they had left the pyramid. Ra silently thanked his followers and worshipers for giving him power.

A scream vibrated through the darkness of the tunnel again. Everyone turned to face the shadows.

"What was that?" Linx asked.

"If I knew, I would've told you by now," Haydeez answered.

Linx scoffed. "Thanks, love. That's helpful."

Footsteps whispered from the shadows.

"No," Haydeez said. "He's here. We can't let him in here, Linx. We have to get him outside before she sees him."

"What about her?" he asked as he nodded down to Pandora's daughter. "We can't leave her here."

Haydeez sighed. "You're going to have to drag her out of here. It's our only option. I'll stop him from coming down the tunnel. You get her outside."

Linx shook his head. "She won't make it down the mountain, love. We barely made it up here."

"We don't have time to argue, Linx!" Haydeez snapped. "Just do the best you can. None of us can be in here when Ra traps her. Just do it. I'll deal with the son." She pushed herself up and started into the darkness.

Linx took a deep breath and groaned. "Right. I'll just do it then," he mumbled to himself. He glanced up at Ra and asked, "How much time do I have?"

"You must move quickly, child. When it happens, it will be fast," Ra answered calmly. A soft glow edged around his body. He looked at peace.

Haydeez moved along the wall quietly. The footsteps grew louder. A figure came into view. Haydeez stuck her arm out and knocked the person to the ground.

He landed with a thud and a grunt. "Who's there?" he asked.

"You need to get out of here. You can't be in this cave," Haydeez said. "If you don't leave on your own, I will force you out of here."

The man shook his head. "I don't even know why I'm here but I feel like I have to be. I tried not to come but," he paused. "It was like my body moved on its own." He moved his head to look around but shadows were all he saw. "Who are you?"

"I'm the one that's going to make sure you're not in this cave in the next ten minutes or less," she whispered close to his ear. She stood up and stepped back. "Let's go."

The man pulled himself up and tried to turn towards the mouth of the cave. "I can't," he said. "I can't turn around. Something won't let me. Why can't I turn around?" he asked with a quiver in his voice. "What's wrong with me?"

Haydeez sighed. "Ok, so this is going to be harder than I hoped." She grabbed the man by the arm and pulled him towards the entrance.

He planted his feet and yanked his arm back. "I'm so sorry. I don't know why I did that," he said. "Why can't I control my own body?"

She grabbed his arm. "Let's try this again," she said. Her fingers dug into his flesh. "We're leaving." Her muscles tensed as she pulled.

The man yelled in pain. "Stop! You're going to break my arm!"

Her nails broke the skin and drew blood. "Why won't you move?" she yelled.

He jerked his arm back and touched the tiny cuts. "I'm bleeding. What the heck is happening?" he yelled.

"I don't know!" she yelled back. "But you need to leave or you'll die!"

• • •

Linx grabbed the woman by the arms and began to drag her into the darkness. "I'm really sorry about this," he mumbled. He pulled her along the stone, through the dirt and shadows. "I hope this works. If it doesn't, we're all dead." He grunted. "Are you stuck on something?" he asked.

Her body had stopped and Linx dropped her arm. He bent down next to her and felt around on the ground. "You're not caught on anything. Why did we stop?" he asked. With her hand in his once more, he stood up and tried to pull again. The pair did not move an inch. "This is not good." He turned to face the entrance. "We're not even close. There's no way we'll get out in time." With a glance back to the cavern, he added, "I have to tell him not to start yet. We won't survive."

A scream echoed off the walls and Linx spun around. "Bloody hell. Guess you're staying here for now," he said and placed her arm on the floor. With his hand on the wall, he made his way towards the entrance. The further he went, the louder the storm became outside. He saw two figures ahead.

"Haydeez, are you alright?" he asked.

She responded with a grunt and a groan. "I can't get him out of the cave, Linx. I can't pull him away. What's going on?"

Linx shook his head. "I don't know. I can't get the other one out either. I got her into the tunnel and then it's like she's caught on something. She's still unconscious but I can't get her passed that point. I don't know what to do."

Haydeez sighed. "We have to do something. How much time do we have?"

"Less than ten minutes."

Chapter 27

Pandora panted heavily like a dog left out in the heat. She doubled over in pain and clutched her eyes. A smear of blood streaked across her cheek.

The phenix egg sat quietly on the ground at her feet. The heat that had permeated the cavern had begun to dissipate and the icy air from outside had already started to creep into the tunnel.

With all the energy she had already released, Pandora was concerned that she did not have enough to complete her task. For the first time since she took over Eve's body, she began to doubt herself. "Doubt is for humans," she said to herself. "I cannot doubt myself. I cannot allow myself to succumb to these simple human emotions. This must happen. I am so close." She took a deep breath and filled her lungs. The air slowly slipped passed her lips in an attempt to calm her body. With her next deep breath, Pandora slowly stood up. "You will die with your pets," she said. "I have offered you too many opportunities to join my side. You can only smack me away so many times. You will watch your friends die and when all of man takes its last breath, I will then take yours."

Pandora lifted her hand. The phenix egg rose with it. It floated in front of her. She closed her eyes and began to chant again.

A slow breeze began to blow around her once more. Warm waves started to ripple off of her body and crawl out across the black water.

· · ·

Ra watched Linx drag Pandora's daughter into the tunnel and then looked at the disc. The white stone in the middle was no longer cloudy. It was almost clear with little gold rivers throughout. It felt light in his hand as if he held a piece of fluff. "I never believed that I would be here at this point, however, we created this for a reason." His fingers closed around the disc and he stood up.

He watched Pandora's body straighten as he began to walk around the edge of the cavern towards her.

"It is time to go, child. Your purpose is no longer of any value to us. The humans have evolved. We have evolved," Ra said calmly. "You are finished. You must either evolve beyond your fundamental purpose or," he paused. "You must go away forever. I will give you a choice, child. However, I will not give you much time to make your decision." He held out his empty hand towards Pandora. "What will you do, child?"

Pandora opened her eyes and shadows spilled out. Her eyes were completely black now. The darkness oozed out and rolled down her cheeks slowly like a thick tar. It covered the dried blood and dripped off her face. The dense liquid landed on the ground in heavy plops. "Father, are you not proud of me? After all this time, I am finally able to fulfill my purpose. Are you not pleased? You and all the others? I have overcome so many obstacles to arrive at this moment, father. Surely you are satisfied with me now?" she asked.

Ra shook his head. "Child, your time is done. You have made your decision and now I must proceed," he answered with a sigh. "We had all hoped to never reach this precipice. No parent wishes to destroy their own children," he paused. "Or so we believed. Your desire to do harm to your children has shown me that you have moved beyond your purpose to obsession. Your heart is haunted. This path will only lead to pain. Once your children are destroyed, what will be your purpose, child? What will you do? Have you asked yourself these questions?" Ra asked Pandora. His feet hovered above the dirt and his glow pulsed all around him.

"There is no need to worry about what happens next. My purpose will be fulfilled. There is nothing more for me to do," she answered calmly. The egg floated behind her. It began to hum. "My children are here now. Questions are pointless. I have everything I need to destroy man. Everything is here, father. Join me and together we will build a world for our kind to once again rule!"

"It is over, child," Ra said. He stood in the middle of the path, his fingers closed tightly around the disc. "It is time for you to go." He closed his eyes and tilted his head back. The soft glow began to grow in intensity. It pulsed and stretched like a sheet. Ra began to chant under his breath.

Pandora shook her head. "No, you will not take this from me," she growled. "You created me to accomplish this and now you stand in my way?" She shouted. "I will destroy man!"

Heat exploded all around her. The waters began to bubble and pop. It crashed and pulsed like waves in a terrible storm. The phenix egg glowed with a heat of its own and steam rose from the delicate shell.

Haydeez and Linx spun towards the cavern. "Pandora," she said. "We have to get them out of here!"

"They won't move," Linx said as panic crept into his voice. "I'm not dying in here, love. And I'm not letting you die either. We need to tell Ra to wait until we get them out."

"I'll go back," she said. "Just keep him from going any further. Don't let him get around you." She ran towards the glow of the cavern before Linx could stop her.

Linx turned to the man. "Don't make this difficult, mate," he said.

"I can't make a promise. It's taking all my strength to just stand here," the man answered. "I don't know how much longer I can stop myself."

Linx nodded. "I can see that, well, sort of see. It's so dark in here. I can barely see you at all. By the way, what's your name, mate?"

"You may call me Father Armo," the man answered. He stuck his hand out into the darkness in an attempt to shake hands.

Linx reached out and grasped his hand. "Of course you're a priest," he mumbled. "You can call me Linx, mate. I'm hopefully here to save your life. Although right now I'm not sure how that's going to happen."

Father Armo chuckled and took a step. He gasped and said, "That's not good."

"Just stay there, Father," Linx said. He stepped in front of the priest and put his hands up. "No more steps. Don't laugh, don't talk. Don't do anything that breaks your concentration."

Father Armo nodded without a word.

Haydeez raced past Pyrrha's body as it sat motionless in the dirt. She did not bother to check on the woman. Her mind was focused on Ra. "Please tell me you didn't start yet," she mumbled to herself. The light from Ra's body lit the cavern before her. "Ra! We can't get out!" she shouted.

She slid to a halt when she saw the scene on the path.

Black shadows oozed from Pandora's eyes and a halo of white light surrounded Ra's massive frame. "I'm too late," she said as she watched Ra's lips move. A heavy breath escaped her lips like all the wind had been knocked out of her lungs. "No," was all she could say.

The egg began to spin. Fire cracked through the shell as tiny pieces fell to the floor.

"You are too late, father," Pandora's voice boomed. "There is no way to stop me. I will succeed and you will be proud of me! You will all be proud of me finally!" Heat flooded the cavern and knocked Haydeez back a couple steps. "Come to me, children! Come home to me!" she shouted.

•   •   •

Pyrrha's body shuddered on the ground in the dark tunnel. Her eyes remained closed as she lifted herself up. Her limbs appeared to move through other means, like a marionette on an intricate series of strings and rods. Her body still moved towards the cavern despite each step being forced and mechanical.

Father Armo took a deep breath and let it out slowly. He closed his eyes for a moment in silent prayer.

Linx stood with his hands still raised, frozen in place, in case the priest moved again. He could barely see but he knew where the man was and stayed vigilant.

With a gasp, Father Armo's head snapped up and his eyes opened wide. "No," he whispered. With a grunt and a groan, he tried to fight the tether that tightened. "Something's wrong," he said. "Something's pulling me."

His leg dragged through the dirt as he fought against the tension. "Lord, help me."

Linx pressed his hands against the priest's chest and pushed back. It was like his hands were against a steel beam secured in the ground. "No, you can't go back there. We're all going to die if you do!" he yelled. "You have to fight it!" He leaned his whole body into it and began to slide backwards. "No! Fight it, Father! She's going to kill you!"

The more Linx pushed, the more ground he lost. He could feel the heat on his back from the cavern and he knew that he was close. "Haydeez, I can't stop him!" he yelled. "Help!"

Tears streamed down Father Armo's cheeks. "I'm so sorry, son. I can't fight it. I don't know what to do. Tell me what to do," he pleaded. "Lord, tell me what to do!" His eyes were wide and his lip trembled. His movements looked broken and painful. He refused to give in to the invisible puppet master. No matter the agony he felt, Father Armo would fight to stay away from whatever waited for him at the end of the tunnel.

•　　•　　•

Pandora chuckled. "They are here. My children are here to play their part in the destruction of man! Welcome, children," she said with her arms wide. She took several deep breaths. "It is time for your sacrifice," she added.

Pyrrha stumbled into the cavern, eyes still closed.

Haydeez spun around just as Father Armo pushed Linx through the entrance. "Linx, are you alright?" she asked.

"Just peachy, love," he grunted. "Slight problem though." He turned quickly. He shoved his shoulder into the priest's chest and dug his heels into the dirt. "Can't seem to stop moving."

Everything appeared to slow down as Haydeez looked between Linx, Pandora, and Ra. She could feel her breath catch in her throat. Her heart banged against her rib cage. "What do I do?" she breathed. "I can't save everyone." Her mind raced as she tried to figure out the best possible solution. Someone would die no matter she did. She had to decide who would lose their life and who would walk out of here. "I can't do this." She turned back to Ra. "Tell me what to do! You're a god. Fix this!" she yelled.

Ra lifted his face to the roof of the cavern. He chanted to himself.

Haydeez had to turn away. The glow became too intense for her to look directly at him. She turned back to Linx. His heels were in the dirt but Father Armo continued to push. She went to Pyrrha who stood, unconscious, against a wall. Her body had not moved in a while but she was still alive. "Linx! Bring him here!" Haydeez yelled.

"I'll try," Linx grunted. He looked at the priest. "Think we can try to move over that way, Father?"

The priest nodded. He clenched his jaw and focused his attention on Haydeez and Pyrrha. His body turned slightly and he took a step. "It doesn't hurt if I don't fight it," he said. "Maybe that's where I'm supposed to be. Perhaps God wants me to go to her."

Linx nodded. "I'm going to let you go now. Keep walking towards them. Ok?" he said.

Father Armo nodded quickly.

Linx jumped to the side. He held his hands up to block the priest in case he tried to walk in the wrong direction, but each step took them closer to the two women.

Haydeez reached out and took Father Armo's hand. "I need you to stay with her. You can't leave her under any circumstances. You have to hold her hand, or better yet, put your arms around her and don't let go, understand?" she asked breathlessly. "This is end-of-the-world important. We can't get you out of this cave in time. That egg," she paused and pointed to the phenix egg. "That's keeping you here. It called you here. I can't explain it all right now but you're the reason humanity keeps going. If you two die apart, we all die. So you absolutely have to hold onto her as if the earth depended on it."

"Because it does," Father Armo sighed. "I don't actually understand any of this right now. It's not making sense but then again," he stopped and looked around. "God works in mysterious ways. I promise you that I will not let her go." He stepped forward and wrapped his arms around Pyrrha.

Pyrrha gasped and her eyes flew open. "It's time. We have to die now," she said calmly and looked up at her brother. "I'm glad you finally got here, Graecus. I was afraid you would not make it in time. But you're here now." She paused, her brow furrowed. "We weren't supposed to die yet, but as long as we're here together, the earth will survive," she added with a smile.

Father Armo looked at Pyrrha, eyes wide. His mouth hung open as if he was ready to say something but could not remember the words. He gasped and dug his fingers into Pyrrha's back. Sweat began to form on his forehead as he tried to catch his breath. Finally, his shoulders relaxed and he sighed. "I'm sorry to worry you. I'm sorry you had to go through such pain. I will always find you in time." He smiled back and hugged her close. "You are weak. You don't have much time." He turned to Haydeez. "I will not leave her."

Haydeez nodded and turned to Linx. "We need to go now." She motioned back to Ra. "I have no idea how much time we have." She looked him in the eyes and added, "We may not even have time to make it out of here."

Linx took her hand and said, "Then I suggest we run."

Chapter 28

Heat poured out of the egg and began to boil the water. The flames spilled out from the crack but did not fall to the floor. They snaked out into the air and spread. A loud crack echoed off the stone as the egg split open.

Fire swirled and spun in the air over the water. It rolled and twisted until two flames split off the sides. They looked like two fire ropes. The center fed the outstretched arms. Feathers began to sprout and grow into a beautiful pair of blazing wings that stretched out to over ten feet. Through all the flames, a head formed. It rose up, pale blue eyes open. The creature swung its head back and screeched.

Everyone in the cavern turned towards the sound.

"Is that a bloody phoenix?" Linx asked.

"Phenix, my son," Ra said calmly. "That would be a phenix. It is here to bring the children to their next life."

Pandora chuckled. "No. It is here to die. You see, I needed to amass enough power to crack the egg open before its time. In order to do that, the egg had to call together my children. Unfortunately for them, they will still die. But then, so will the rest of man," she said. "The egg could not be opened until both of my children were present. Now that they are, my plan will be completed." She turned to the phenix and smiled. "You must now die for the last time."

Ra spun the dials on the disc and turned towards Pandora. "You had your chance, child. Please remember that," he said.

The stone swirled once again like it had done so many times before today. A bright white glow circled around each dial. The symbols that Ra had lined up sparked to life. It looked like tiny bolts of lightning traced each ancient rune.

"No!" Pandora shouted. "You will not win, father. This is my whole being. It is why I am here!" She raised her hand with what looked like a glob of the thick, black water. "Do not fret, phenix. This will be concluded quickly. I must tell you that you will feel a great deal of pain." She pulled her hand back as if to pitch a ball. "Brace yourself," she added and threw the black blob at the creature.

It screeched and turned in the air with ease. Its blue eyes grew even lighter than they already were as it eyed Pandora.

"They're over here!" Haydeez shouted and waved at the fire creature.

Linx stood with his eyes wide. "What are you doing?" he asked.

"It needs to take them now before Pandora can do anything. If we can get them safe, we can get out of this stupid cave," she answered.

Linx nodded quickly. "Good point." He turned back toward the creature. It hovered over the water with its eyes fixed on them. "It doesn't think we're a threat, right?" he asked.

Haydeez shook her head. "It shouldn't," she answered. "But I could be wrong," she added with a shrug.

A low hum vibrated through the cavern. "You must leave now, child, before it is too late," Ra said to Haydeez. "You are running out of time."

"I have to make sure the phenix takes them. I can't leave till I know they're gone," she shouted.

Linx grabbed her arm. "We have to go now, love!" he yelled.

The ground rumbled as the wind swirled around them. Dirt and pebbles spun through the air. Haydeez squinted. "What if it doesn't take them? We die anyway. Just go. I'll stay here to make sure." She pulled her arm from his grasp. "We can't risk it."

Ra spun the last dial and said, "Now would be the time." His voice boomed over the howl of the wind.

Pandora growled. "Move, father!" she shouted. "I have work to complete! I will not be stopped!" She stepped towards Ra and slipped on the loose ground. She smacked her hands into the dirt and screamed. "Move!" The waters erupted into the air as if an explosion went off beneath the surface.

The phenix circled Pandora's children and squawked.

Linx pointed and said, "Can we leave now?"

Haydeez watched the creature for a moment and took a step towards the tunnel. "Run!" she yelled at Linx.

Without another word, they took off into the darkness.

The phenix settled onto the children and a soft glow covered the three of them.

"No!" Pandora screamed. "I called you so I could destroy you. You will not be reborn!" She thrust her hands towards her children and the winds followed. They were knocked to the ground in a heap. The phenix tumbled to the wall. "I will kill you no matter what it takes."

Ra's body glowed white. The gem inside the disc was just a blur of motion. Lightning arched around the stone. "I have unlocked the gates, my child. Now you must enter," he said calmly.

A bolt of lightning leapt from the center of the dial and grabbed onto Pandora like a hand. She shrieked in pain but kept her eyes focused on her children. "You cannot take this from me, father! This is why you made me!" She twisted and squirmed.

Pyrrha reached for her brother. "Graecus, take my hand. This body is too weak for me to move on my own. I need your help," she said.

Graecus reached for his sister. "I will not leave you," he said and pulled her close. A large blood spot had appeared on his knee. He looked around the cave and found the phenix. It was on the floor, wings spread wide. It did not move much, but he could see it was still alive. He knew that once it turned to ash, there was no way to save the two of them. He scooted along the ground and pulled Pyrrha along with him. One leg hung limply as he used the other to push himself through the dirt. "We need to reach the creature. It's the only way for us to be reborn. I'm so sorry to drag you along the ground, Pyrrha," he said and pulled her further.

Pyrrha smiled up at her brother. "Don't worry. None of this will matter soon," she said. "You will not only save us, you will save humanity. I could never be angry at that." With her free hand, she used as much strength as she could pull together and touched Graecus's arm. "I, and the whole of humanity, will be forever indebted to you, my brother."

Ra whispered another chant and the cavern exploded into a blinding light. "When the door closes, you will need to be under the phenix wing," he said to Pyrrha and Graecus. "The blast will kill you for certain."

Pandora howled in pain as the light burned her skin. She threw her head back and tears streamed down her cheeks. "No! I cannot lose! What will happen to me?" she cried. Her body began to shake as the sobs overtook her.

"You will be trapped for eternity, my child. You will not be able to hurt your children any longer," Ra answered calmly. "You had a choice, child, and you made it. You must live with your decision."

The lightning began to pull Pandora towards Ra. She dug her heels into the dirt and fought against the strength of the spell, but her body had used up the energy she had syphoned from the creatures. Every muscle tensed and shook as she tried to stop the pull of the lightning. Tears poured from her eyes and ran down to her neck. The neckline of her shirt was soaked with salty fluid, but she refused to give in and let it take her.

Graecus pulled Pyrrha as quickly as he could to the phenix. He reached out to touch the wing and slid his sister underneath. The fire did not hurt him, but it did begin to burn his flesh. "This will be over soon, sister. We are safe." He moved his body close to Pyrrha under the phenix wing and they held each other tight. The light from the disc had covered every inch of the cavern except under the wing. They just looked into each other's eyes and waited for death. The phenix stretched its wing over them completely and just sat in silence.

Chapter 29

"I can hear the wind. Let's go!" Haydeez shouted.

"I can see the moonlight. How far do we have to go?" Linx asked between breaths.

Haydeez shrugged. "No idea. Just keep running and hope we're out of range," she answered.

A blast of icy air knocked them back a couple steps. They looked at each other and groaned. The wind howled as snow and ice pounded against the side of the cliff. Their faces stung as tiny bits flew through the air to crash into their exposed skin.

Linx looked down into the darkness below. "Looks a bit familiar," he yelled. He turned to the path. "Bloody hell, it's practically gone. How are we getting down now?"

Haydeez pulled her zipper all the way up and tugged her gloves a little further up her wrist. "Race you to the bottom!" she yelled with a laugh. "Don't fall off the mountain just because it's the fastest way down!" She started to pick her steps, carefully but quickly, down the path.

"Race? Are you mad? I'll be lucky if I make it down to solid ground!" he yelled after her. With a quick glance back at the cave entrance, he turned and followed her.

Each step had to be calculated and precise or they would slip over the side of the cliff into the darkness that waited below. There would be no recovering the body at that point. The snow would take them.

Fortunately for the pair, the winds pounded against the cliff and forced them close to the mountain. Haydeez walked with her face barely a hair from the frozen cliff. Her breath no longer came out in warm little puffy clouds. The frozen air had stolen most of the warmth from her body, but she continued to move. It filled her lungs and threatened to freeze her from the inside out. She knew she had to move as far away as possible. She could feel the energy build in the air and did not want to be around when it was released.

Linx was close behind. Tiny chunks of ice and snow stuck to his eyebrows. He squinted to keep his eyes on Haydeez. They both knew that, even if one was knocked off the cliff, there was nothing the other would be able to do.

Without warning, the whole cliff began to shake. Snow and ice fell from above onto the pair. Haydeez reached back and grabbed for Linx. She flattened herself against the cliff and closed her eyes. She felt Linx press his arm across her shoulders with all his strength. His body was right next to her. Her face was ice cold against the cliff. She tried to steady her breath and calm her heart but the vibrations were too much.

A boom rocked the path and threatened to throw them into the shadows below. Linx closed his eyes tight as he pushed Haydeez as close to the side of the cliff as possible. He clenched his teeth and pressed his cheek to the icy rock.

Haydeez hunched her shoulders. "Please be over. Don't let us die," she mumbled to herself, over and over. She gripped the front of Linx's coat with one hand and hugged the wall with the other. Her gloves were covered in snow and almost frozen to the cliff. The winds pounded their backs and forced them closer to the mountain. Haydeez had to take shallow quick breaths because the pressure was too much to fill her lungs. She felt like her chest was stuck under a truck. "Please let it be over. I don't want to die," she mumbled.

●　　　●　　　●

The floor of the cavern began to rumble and shake. Ra held the disc tight in his hands as the lightning pulled one last time. It dragged Pandora into the cloudy gem in the middle of the disc. Her body became limp and fell to the ground. Her essence folded in on itself as the lightning tightened and squeezed until Pandora was a mere speck of her former self. The lightning disappeared into the gem with Pandora.

Her cage snapped shut with a boom. The explosion sent a wave of energy to the walls of the cavern and through the tunnel.

Pandora's children lay huddled under the massive wing of the phenix bird as the wave swept over them. Their bodies began to crumble and wither until nothing was left but ash. The phenix bird exploded into a cloud of embers and smoke. Tiny sparks bounced between the piles of ashes and pulled them together. What remained of the two children and the creature was now a singular pile the size of an ostrich egg.

The sparks danced around in a pattern. They leapt and raced over the heap to create a shell. Thin red lines traced their way across the snow white surface of the egg.

When the dance was complete, Ra reached down and lifted the phenix egg. "Your cycle has been sustained. Keep them safe until they are reborn, creature," he said calmly. "Your work will be completed soon. Then you may rest again." He ran his fingers over the deceptively resilient shell. "Your next life will not have such an abrupt ending, my poor grandchildren. I will ensure that your life will be long and happy." The god cradled the egg in his arm and turned to the husk left behind when Pandora's essence was removed. He bent down, lifted the body easily with one hand, and carried it to the water.

Ra looked at the shiny black surface as the waves began to calm. "Your choice to accept Pandora was not made with ill intent. Your innocence made you a perfect target for her. Your body may rest and become one with the earth once again. Your soul is freed, child," he said as he bent down and placed the body into the water.

Bubbles and steam rose to pull Eve's body into the depths beneath. She rested on the surface for a moment as if she were on solid ground. Then the water tugged her down. A white puff escaped her lips before the darkness swallowed her.

With the egg nestled against his chest, Ra walked towards the tunnel.

The black inky waters were quiet once again.

Chapter 30

"Is it over yet?" Linx asked through clenched teeth. His eyes were still closed tight and his muscles ached from how long he had held Haydeez against the cliff. He refused to loosen his grip.

Haydeez peeked over her shoulder. Her breath caught in her throat. She shook Linx by the front of his jacket, where she still had a death grip. "What the.... You have got to see this," she said. Her eyes were wide as she looked out over the snow towards the horizon.

Linx managed to pull his eyes open and slowly turned. "Bloody hell. What happened?" he asked. "Where's the storm?"

Haydeez shrugged. "I have no idea," she answered. "It's like that island again."

The clouds had cleared. They could see out over the island. The snow had already begun to slow and quietly fell onto the ground. Stars peeked out between the clouds in the night sky.

"Wow, I guess it's night now," Linx joked.

"This is crazy," Haydeez said. "It's like someone turned off the blender. The ice is still there but it's not flying around, crashing into things anymore."

Linx chuckled. "Probably the most accurate description you could've made at the moment. So, are we dead?" he asked with a smirk.

Haydeez scoffed. "You think this is the afterlife?"

With a laugh, he said, "So, we did it. We actually stopped Pandora." He took a deep breath and let it out slowly. "What do you think happened to her kids?"

"They are resting before the next birth," Ra said. He moved quietly down the path. His body still gave off a glow but he was not as tall anymore. "The phenix protected them under its wing. The poor creature almost lost its life before I was able to take their lives. It took quite a hit when Pandora blasted it." He motioned to the egg. "When her cage slammed shut, the explosion ended their latest cycle as the bird lost its light."

Haydeez and Linx stood in awe. Ra did not have a bit of dirt on his body or clothing. He did not look like a god who had just battled his own child to save humanity. "None of this feels real," Haydeez said. "It's so hard to believe that it's over, that Pandora is gone. I'm exhausted but I don't know how to feel right now. It's like a major part of your life is over all of the sudden. How am I supposed to feel right now?"

Linx put his arm around her shoulders and squeezed. "Take the win, love. Take it and run. We're done with her. It's over. We can take a bit of a break now and relax," he said with a smile.

"But what happens to everything that was let out?" Haydeez asked.

Ra nodded. "There are the evils that had to be released upon the earth, of course. Fortunately, the worst ones need a willing host and without a body, well, they are not capable of asking," Ra answered. "You will probably hunt some of the smaller evils. However, the greater ones will remain a faded memory of history." He handed Haydeez the disc. "You will no longer fight at her whim."

Haydeez took the disc and turned it over in her hands. "This little piece of gold opens doors to other realms?" she asked and looked into Ra's eyes. "And you want to trust me with it? How do you know I'll protect it? How do you know I won't do something to let her out? I don't even know what to do with this."

Ra smiled and took her hand. "You have fought hard to stop her. You would have given your life to ensure the survival of all humans. Yes, I trust you. I have no reason to doubt your capabilities. You will keep it secure. She will not be released again. Does this answer your questions?"

"You left out what to do with it," Linx chimed in.

Ra nodded. "Of course. The disc must remain in a pine box. I will give you an inscription for it. Once completed, it will not be unlocked or broken without a counter spell," he answered.

Haydeez sighed heavily. "Then I guess it's finally done." She looked around and expected something else to happen.

The air was once again quiet and peaceful. A breeze knocked some snow from above. It tumbled down into the piles below with a plop.

Linx looked out over all the white and said, "I wonder how long this ice age will last."

Chapter 31

"I know that you're less than pleased with me at the moment, but I did say that I would continue to search for Ra's ship," Cornelius said. "Since you've succeeded, as I knew you would, I have called to share the location with you."

Haydeez sighed. "Ok, so where is it?"

Cornelius cleared his throat. "The ship is on display in the Giza Solar Boat Museum. You're looking for the Khufu Ship. When it was discovered originally, it had been disassembled. To this day, people still speculate what it was actually used for because it has no rigging and no room for paddling. It's known as a solar barge which is meant to carry their pharaoh across the heavens with the sun god himself." He paused. "So, you just have to get him to his ship and the rest is up to him."

"After everything that's happened, it's nice to have an easy task," Linx joked. "We were about due for one."

"Are you sure it will be that easy?" Night Raven asked. "In my experience, nothing is ever that easy."

Haydeez nodded. "I can only hope that it is. This whole thing has been exhausting. So, is there something he has to say or do?"

"I will handle that part," Ra interjected. "Once I am near, it will reveal itself for what it really is."

Linx clapped his hands together and asked, "Well then, shall we get to it?"

"Ready when you are," Checkmate said.

Haydeez shook her head. "Not a chance. We're already going at night to avoid as many people as possible. We don't need all of us going. We don't even know what's going to happen."

"So, we're sidelined again," Checkmate scoffed. "I'm fine. I'm healed. I can go, especially if we're just returning him to his ship. We can't possibly come across anything big and bad at this point."

Linx scrunched his nose. "Those kind of words usually bring the baddies to us. It's probably best if you don't come along."

Checkmate stood with her mouth open. "Seriously? You've got to be kidding me."

"Well, you did almost lose your soul. It's probably smart to take a little time to recuperate. You don't know if there are any long term effects from what she did," Haydeez said. "Just take it easy for a few days. Enjoy the time off. If your boss asks, I promise to tell him you were following me the whole time." She smiled.

"You're not funny." Checkmate turned to Night Raven. "Let me guess. You agree."

He nodded. "You could've died, lokon. Not from a bullet or a stab wound. That thing took your soul." He lowered his voice. "She took you to hell. Stepping back for a moment is acceptable. You're allowed to take a break."

"I know what she did. I was there," she said through gritted teeth. "I need to do something so I don't lose myself in all of it. It's not a want. It's a need." She took him by the hand and whispered, "I need to be here, so my mind doesn't go back there."

Haydeez looked away. It felt awkward and wrong to watch their exchange. She understood more than she wanted to admit. Her eyes fixed on the carpet fibers as thoughts raced through her mind. Finally, she said, "Look, why don't I get you a room here. Top floor. You can stay a few days and relax on me." She walked over to Checkmate and looked her in the eye. "If I were in your position, I would fight to keep my freedom. I would fight to get back out there and hit something to make the pain go away. And I would lose. It doesn't make it go away. Stay here, talk to him about it. Get it out. Say the words to make it real, and then know that she's gone. She can't get you again. I can't make it go away but I can help you heal from it."

Checkmate just stared back at Haydeez for what seemed like hours. Her eyes glistened for a moment before she blinked it away. "Fine. We'll stay here."

Haydeez held the door open and motioned for Ra to step out of the car. "Are you ready to go home?" she asked. The light spilled out onto the dark sand.

"After being held captive in the darkness, unable to see the smallest sliver of light," he paused and closed his eyes. His skin glowed softly, like a child's nightlight. He breathed in deep and sighed. "Yes, child, I am ready to return home." He looked out across the shadowy sand and smiled. With the phenix egg in hand, he stepped away from the car.

Haydeez closed the door. "How close do we need to be?" she asked and started to walk towards the museum.

Before Ra could answer, every window exploded out. Glass rained down on the sand and stone. A hole opened up in the roof of the museum as a polished piece of wood poked through into the moon's glow. Light flooded the hole and spilled out onto the roof.

Haydeez backpedaled and almost fell onto the ground as she crouched. "I guess we don't need to be that close," she said.

The ship pushed its way through the hole in the roof as if the entire building were made of tissue paper.

Haydeez and Linx stared at the museum as the rest of the boat forced its way out. A screech and a scrape echoed off the pyramid. The solar barge slid across the roof and dropped down to the ground. "Yeah, good thing nobody was here to notice that," Linx said.

The glow from the boat intensified quickly until there was nothing left but a massive ball of white.

Linx covered his eyes and turned away. "Bloody hell! What's happening?" he shouted.

"It's beautiful," Haydeez said as she stared at Ra's solar barge. "It's so much more beautiful than I imagined it would be. Linx, isn't it amazing?" she asked, her eyes focused on the glow.

Linx tried to turn but quickly shielded his eyes again. "I can't see a bloody thing! It's burning my eyes, love." He took a step back and fell to the ground. He rolled over and tried to bury his face in the sand to protect his vision.

Haydeez smiled to herself and unclenched her fists. The light washed over her and flowed into her eyes. "This is where you live?" she asked.

Before her on the sand was a golden ship. She wondered for a moment if it could even be called a ship without those distinct features. Her thoughts passed quickly to the majesty in front of her. Every inch of the ship reflected the inner glow back out. There was a wave of light that constantly rolled off the sides only to disappear into a cloudy mist beneath. It sat on a thick cloud of fog, but the sand beneath remained dry. She wanted to reach out to touch it. As she stepped forward, her hand moved to the polished, gilded planks. "Why aren't they hot?" she asked.

Ra chuckled. "There is so much more to you than you know, child. I wish I could see your true self. I do not know what is hiding it, but I hope that it reveals itself to you someday," he said. He stepped towards the ship and a small plank opened up. As he stepped aboard, he turned. "Would you like to come aboard for a moment?" he asked.

Haydeez gasped. She covered the steps between herself and the plank quickly. As her feet met the deck, the energy raced through her body. Shivers rippled up and down her arms as goosebumps danced across her skin. A breath caught in her throat as she tried to speak, but the words would not come. She just stared at everything and tried to commit it all to memory. Not only was there no mast or rudder, but the lack of a wheel caused her to pause as well.

When she finally found her voice, she asked, "How does it go?"

"Through my will alone does this barge travel," Ra answered. "Thank you, child, for not only freeing me, but for returning me to it. I am once again in my rightful place. I can feel my people once more. Soon, I will be in the sky again, where I belong."

Haydeez turned to Ra. "After everything that I have learned or heard about gods, I expected you to be much more," she paused. "Much more angry. I guess people have always been taught that the head of a pantheon is an angry, vengeful man. So far, the two I've met have been pretty chill and incredibly accommodating. I don't know what to make of that."

Ra smiled. "There are vengeful gods. There are those who would strike down a human for speaking of another or thinking of worshiping another. I, however, am not one of those gods. I provide for my worshipers and protect them from those angry beings," he answered. He motioned to the plank. "I must return to the skies, child. I cannot thank you enough for what you have done. I will protect the egg until it is time for the children to meet again. It will be safe here."

Haydeez stepped off the barge and turned to face Ra again. "Thank you for working with me. If you hadn't helped, we would all be gone by now. I think I need a new charm on my necklace now," she said and touched the tiny silver pieces. "I'm missing a sun disk." She smiled at Ra and stepped backwards.

The plank disappeared back into the side of the barge and melded seamlessly into the wood.

Ra smiled. "Find your true self, child. Once you do, it will free you." He bowed his head slightly as the barge rose off the sand.

"You know, with everything you've done to help us, I'm not even going to be mad about you saying that," she said with a chuckle. She bowed her head in return and waved.

As the glow faded into the stars, Haydeez finally turned to find Linx curled up on the ground behind her. "What's up, little ostrich? Why is your head in the sand?" she asked.

Linx groaned. "I can't see, love. I think I'm permanently blind," he said. He rolled over with his arm across his eyes. "Why is it so bright?"

Haydeez laughed. "What are you talking about?"

"The barge, it was like looking directly into the sun if the sun were right here in front of me. How are you not blind?" he asked.

"I didn't even notice the light," she answered. "It was super shiny and sparkled a lot but it didn't seem all that bright to me." She pushed his foot with hers. "By the way, he's gone. You can probably uncover your eyes now. We might want to leave the area before someone shows up. That was a loud explosion and I don't know how close we are to people." She reached down and grabbed his hand. "Let's go, you big baby. Time to get moving." She yanked him up onto his feet. "You're ok to drive, right?" she joked.

Linx grunted as he stood up. "You're just so funny." He moved his arm and slowly opened his eyes. "There are tiny white dots on everything. I'll drive if you don't mind dying in a fiery car crash in the desert," he said. "We'll go down in a blaze of hot metal and gasoline. How does that sound?"

Haydeez laughed. "Are you hungry? I'm hungry."

Chapter 32

"I just don't think I can talk to him right now. He says that people are talking about me but won't tell me who. Then, there's the question of where his extensive collection of books comes from and why he's the only one in the world with them," Haydeez said. "Too many questions." She paced in her living room.

Linx stood in front of the fireplace, his back to the cold hearth. "If you want, I can talk to him. That way you don't have to worry about blowing up in his face or breaking something in his house," he said. "I will go alone and find out what's going on. It'll be like my own little mission while you wait at home," he joked.

Haydeez scoffed. "Like you could go on a mission without me."

"I can totally handle myself, thank you. I don't need you to protect me," Linx huffed. "And besides, what is an old man going to do to me? If he wanted to hurt me, he would've done it by now." He walked over to Haydeez and put his arm around her shoulders. "Maybe it's time we trust him. He gave us everything we asked for and then some. He even let you keep that dagger."

"You mean that one that tried to control my brain and then made me pass out twice? That dagger?" she asked.

Linx sighed. "No, love. I mean, the dagger that gave you the ability to take down two different monsters with little to no effort. I get that you're mad at him, but you have to look at the positives. How was he supposed to know that it would do that to you? He could never get it to work. He's invited you to his home to see all of his artifacts. It's like a mystical playground in there. You, of all people, would be able to stop him if he tried to hurt you. You've got the upper hand in just about everything. I'm not saying to go there unarmed. I'm just saying," he paused. "Hear what he has to say and then decide how you feel."

She groaned. "Stop making sense. Can't you just fuel my rage once?"

"That's not how this works, love. I'm supposed to stop you from doing stupid things," Linx said with a smile. "Besides, I don't want to be around when you go absolutely mad. I'll probably be the first to die."

Haydeez thought for a moment. "Well, you've screwed up enough times that my rage would most likely target you first. I mean, come on, I know where you sleep. It's only twenty steps from my bedroom door. I could hunt you and you wouldn't even know it because I already know your routine," she said with a smirk.

"Not funny."

"Then why am I smiling?"

"Because you're a little evil on the inside."

Cornelius sighed. "Look, dear, I've already told you. The books have been in my family since before writing. Some of them don't even contain the English language. As I've stated, you're more than welcome to look through any book you desire, except of course, my personal journal that I keep by the bedside," he said with a smile. "It's a joke, dear. Don't look so angry."

"So, why are you the only one that has these books? Why isn't there another person on this whole planet who knows about this stuff?" she asked.

"What makes you think that nobody else does? Have you read every book in existence? Have you spoken to everyone on this planet? Have you traveled to every library there has ever been? Doubtful. You're skilled but you don't have that kind of time," he answered.

Linx raised an eyebrow and said, "He does kind of have a point. I mean, even with the internet, people still hide things. We can't even figure out where Peter is, let alone look at every book in existence."

Haydeez eyed Linx, a hidden fire behind the calm blue.

He held up his hands. "Hey, don't be angry at me, love. It's true. It's not fair to be angry at him just because he has some rare books. Is it weird? Sure, of course. Do other people we know have rare books too?" he asked.

The fire died down to a few red embers as Linx held her gaze.

"Yes," she answered reluctantly.

"You can't know everything, love," he whispered as he leaned closer. "There will always be things that we can't explain. Just a few months ago neither of us ever thought we'd meet Pandora and a few weeks ago, well, did you know what that serpent leopard thing was? It doesn't even have a name, love. Look, I know you hate to give up control, but sometimes you don't have a choice."

Haydeez huffed, her lips pursed and brow furrowed. She rolled her head back and forth, then sighed. "Fine. I don't have to know everything, but I don't have to be ok with this."

"To be fair, dear, I've been honest with you. I'm not hiding anything. The books and a large portion of the items have been in my family for a long time. Some of the items I've acquired more recently," Cornelius said. "But, for the most part, they're all mine. I can't use them because they don't respond to me. For example, that dagger. I have no use for it, but if you do, well then, I would prefer it to be in the hands of someone doing good things in this world," he said with a shrug. He took a sip of tea and leaned back in his chair.

"How do you make your money if you don't get out much?" she asked.

Cornelius smiled. "Sometimes I loan parts of my collection to museums for a lovely fee. They ignore most of my obscure pieces. Usually they think the pieces are fakes. They prefer the paintings or some of the scale DaVinci models. As long as everything comes back to me, I will continue to make money."

Linx motioned to Cornelius. "See? That makes sense. At least it's not some secret organization like the ones we work with regularly. He probably doesn't even know about The Council."

Cornelius chuckled. "I know enough about them to know that I don't like them at all. And before you ask, no dear, I don't know where they're located. That's one secret they keep hidden quite well. The acquisition of knowledge brings about an increase in control. Unfortunately, they hold the power in this situation."

Linx furrowed his brow and asked, "Did he just quote...? Never mind." He shook his head and added. "He has a point though. The Council holds more power over you than you realize. It's like you let them in your head but forgot to kick them out at the end. You let Peter get under your skin all the time."

"He actually had the nerve to ask me to bring him a live manticore. How are you not more upset about that?" she asked.

"Because I'm not surprised by it," Linx answered. "He's a piece of trash and I always expect him to want a live creature. How are you surprised?"

Haydeez sighed. "I don't know. I just assumed he was smarter than that. My mistake, I guess. I get that he pays me, but I really don't want to talk to him, at least not for a long time. I don't think I can handle listening to his voice."

"Tell him you're taking a break," Cornelius said. "Tell him you'll be taking a much needed vacation after handling, how many jobs did you do for him in Egypt?"

"There were too many," she answered. "I lost track. I can probably check how many deposits were made in my account though." She rolled her shoulders. "A vacation would be nice."

Cornelius took another sip of his tea. "You're welcome to stay here for a while. I know how much you wanted to inspect my collection. There are some pieces in particular that I've been wondering about myself. I'd love to know if they speak to you the way that dagger did. That truly is an interesting phenomenon," he said with a smile.

Linx looked at Haydeez. "That's up to you, love."

"I need to think it over. I'm still not sure how I feel right now. After dealing with Peter so often recently, everything seems to be setting me off," she said. "He really has gotten to me and I need time to get him out of my head. It's just too much right now." She rubbed her face and groaned. "I just need to be in my element for a bit."

Cornelius stood up. "The offer stands." He picked up his cup and motioned to the door. "Shall I show you out? You should probably be heading back home before it's too late. I know it's a long drive." He walked to the door.

Linx shook his head. "She doesn't care about the dark. If her body would let her, she'd drive all night."

The familiar jingle of her phone interrupted the conversation. "Seriously?" she growled. As she pulled the phone out of her pocket, her shoulders relaxed. "It's Joseph. I'll take this outside," she said and began to walk out the door. "Hello?"

Linx shook hands with Cornelius. "Thanks for the help, mate. It might take a while, but the call of those artifacts will be too much for her and she'll have to come back." He smiled. "Take care."

"Safe travels to you both."

Epilogue

A chair smashed into a side table. The table split and crashed to the floor. Splintered wood littered an obscenely expensive rug. Candlelight glittered on the polished pieces. The Venerated One dropped the chair to the floor. His chest rose and fell with heavy breaths. Anger burned in his eyes.

"With all due respect, Venerated One, this is not very becoming. Perhaps we should take a seat and discuss the situation further." The head of La Garduna stood next to a large table with his hands placed on the surface. "We don't want to notify the entire building of your displeasure."

The Venerated One turned and glared at the Spanish man. "Three. There are three of the old gods loose now. Three that our predecessors had captured and taken care of and now, under my watch, they have been released!" he shouted and slammed his fists on the table. "Under my watch! I no longer consider this hunter an asset. She has become a liability and needs to be terminated. We will no longer be contacting her for her so-called services. This is too much."

The other man nodded. "I agree, Venerated One, but should we just stop? She will know that something is amiss. Perhaps we contact her a little less than we did before to ensure that she does not suspect anything out of the ordinary. Then, we can move forward with our plan in private, no eyes on us. She will never suspect anything."

With his hands in his hair, the Venerated One said, "We will do business with her sparingly. What creatures do we have now? We will need to begin their training and reprogramming immediately. The sooner we begin, the sooner she will be finished. I no longer want her out amongst the world. She has already done enough damage." He patted down the stray strands of silver hair and adjusted his coat. "We will bring back order.

Once she is removed, we can begin plans to recapture the gods that have been freed. I will have order again."

"Of course. We will take care of her as soon as the creatures are ready. I will get a list to you at once. I hear we are awaiting the arrival of some new creatures as well." the Spanish man said as he bowed his head. "When she refused to provide us with the manticore, we contacted other hunters to procure other specimens. Once they arrive, we will begin the sessions immediately."

A spark twinkled in his eye as the Venerated One said, "New creatures? How marvelous. Perhaps I should be there when these new beasts arrive."

The conversation stopped as a knock sounded. The two men looked at each other and then eyed the door.

"Enter," the Venerated One said.

As the door slowly opened, a man stood in the doorway dressed in a red cassock and ferraiolo. "Gentlemen," he said, his voice deep and rough. "It has come to my attention that we currently have broken enclosures. Are the animals in the zoo running loose now?" he asked.

The Venerated One stood with his eyes wide. He bowed his head and kissed the man's ring. "Yes, your eminence. There are three animals loose. We were just discussing how to handle..." He began to speak but the cardinal silenced him with a wave of the hand. The Venerated One stepped back and closed his mouth.

"Have you seen the way people now will track creatures for so-called research purposes? How do they choose which ones to monitor and which to ignore? What makes one species more important than the others? It truly is a mystery, is it not?" he asked.

The Venerated One nodded. "Yes, your eminence. It is quite strange. I have never understood how they choose which is more important than the others."

"It's surprisingly simple. You see, I'm the most important. All others are meaningless," the cardinal answered. "What I want and need always comes first. See? Simple," he said matter-of-factly. He stood with his arms tucked into his sleeves. His voice remained calm and relaxed. "Now, what I need is information. There appears to be more happening lately," he paused and looked at the Venerated One. "More than your incompetence, of course." He turned and walked towards the fireplace. "Not only are the animals running free in the zoo, but there are others that are stirring as well."

"Others, your eminence? There are more?" the Venerated One asked. "How many more are loose?"

The cardinal turned. "I love the smell of wood burning, don't you? It's such a lovely scent. I believe that my personal favorite is probably apple wood. I love that light sweet fruity smell. It dulls the smoke and leaves a softer, more palatable, scent after it dies down. Wouldn't you agree?" he asked.

The Spanish council member stood with his mouth open in the shadows. He just watched as the Venerated One tried to make sense of the conversation.

"Yes, your eminence, it is quite a pleasant smell," the Venerated One answered.

"There are four more out there stirring. They're moving and I need to know where. Unfortunately, my sources outside of your Council have not been able to find them as of yet," the cardinal said. "I need to find them before it becomes too late." He eyed the two men. "They cannot be permitted to gather. Now, what I need from you and your silly little Council is for you to find the great dragon mother. She will know where these four are located. You will find her for me and arrange a meeting. That's it. Simple, easy. Even you could handle this."

The Venerated One furrowed his brow. "I don't believe that I understand, your eminence. There are four more gods out there, free? But we have verified that all the other prisons are still intact. How are there four other gods out there that we are not aware of?"

The cardinal chuckled. "Gods? You think there are four more gods out there?" He chuckled again. "You are truly more incompetent than I believed. You have no idea what else is out there do you?"

He bowed his head. "No, your eminence. I don't know what else is out there. I'm sorry to disappoint you. It appears that I have not been privy to necessary information."

The cardinal laughed. He picked up the iron poker and stoked the fire. "It doesn't appear that way. It appears that you haven't taken the initiative to further your knowledge. You focus only on what you're given and not everything else that is out there," he said calmly. "Perhaps you should go back through your beginner's teachings to refresh your memory." He turned to face the two men. "Perhaps your mistake was thinking that you were too good for all of that." He walked up to the Venerated One. His face was so close that he could smell the other man's aftershave. With a smile, he said, "Perhaps pride got in your way."

About the Author

Rebecca has loved writing since she was a little girl. She grew up with a book in each hand. Over the years, the more she read, the more she wanted to write her own book. She finally found the right idea and ran with it. Her character, Haydeez Blackhawk, has allowed her to share stories around the world while looking out over the mountains from her home in eastern TN.

Note from the Author

Word-of-mouth is crucial for any author to succeed. If you enjoyed *Burning Daylight*, please leave a review online—anywhere you are able. Even if it's just a sentence or two. It would make all the difference and would be very much appreciated.

Thanks!
Rebecca Flynn

We hope you enjoyed reading this title from:

BLACK ROSE
writing™

www.blackrosewriting.com

Subscribe to our mailing list – *The Rosevine* – and receive **FREE**
books, daily deals, and stay current with news about upcoming
releases and our hottest authors.
Scan the QR code below to sign up.

Already a subscriber? Please accept a sincere thank you for being a fan of
Black Rose Writing authors.

View other Black Rose Writing titles at
www.blackrosewriting.com/books and use promo code
PRINT to receive a **20% discount** when purchasing.